THE FOUR NATIONS TOURNAMENT

AEGIS OF MERLIN BOOK 6

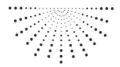

JAMES E WISHER

James E. Wisher

SAND HILL PUBLISHING

WINTER BREAK

The winter wind seemed colder in the Land of the Night Princes. The sun had set hours ago so the locals were up and about. Conryu surveyed the area under the light of a spell globe. He didn't bother with a jacket as his fire magic teacher had been kind enough to show him a spell called Fire Aura. It surrounded him with an invisible energy field that generated heat.

Would've been nice to know the spell this time last year when he was crawling around frozen sewer drains, but school policy said only sophomores and above could learn it.

Stupid rules.

Conryu stood, hands on hips, as a pair of vampires took down the final Imperial tents. The thirty-two witches whose families he'd failed to locate now lived in a refurbished apartment building in one of the many abandoned cities that dotted the country. They'd rigged up generators for power, heat, and to run the water pumps. It would do for the winter. When the weather turned, they'd arrange something more permanent.

He would have liked to find everyone's kin, but most of the older women's parents had died and those still alive barely remembered them. The former White Witches seemed content to live in peace together in the vampires' country. At least their minds were their own again.

The younger witches had been welcomed home with open arms and much crying. Reuniting those families ranked among the most satisfying things Conryu had ever done. When he'd asked, not a single one of them had shown the least interest in studying magic again. Not that he blamed them.

The snow crunched behind him and Talon said, "You should have told us you'd arrived. It's a horrible evening to be standing out in the cold."

As if to emphasize the point a light snow began to fall and sizzle on his fire aura. Prime shook the flakes off his cover and glared all around as if insulted that the precipitation would dare fall on him.

"I only arrived a minute ago and I've learned a trick that keeps the cold from being an issue. I figured when your people saw me they'd tell you I'd arrived. Besides, it's nice out here, peaceful. If ever I need a quiet place to think, I know where to come."

"Yes, if there's one thing we have in abundance, it's quiet." Talon took two more steps until they were side by side. He'd dressed in a formal jacket and tuxedo. Where he'd found one Conryu had no idea. "Are you certain we won't be a burden for your family? It was very generous to invite us to Christmas dinner, but we wouldn't want to impose."

"Relax. I admit my mom was a little leery when I first mentioned I wanted to invite some of my new friends, but once I convinced her the stories were just stories she got into the idea. She even has a surprise dish she made just for you and Sasha that takes into account your unique dietary needs."

Talon raised an eyebrow but refrained from commenting.

"Conryu!" Anya called.

She and her mother were approaching together on foot, each of them dressed in white gowns trimmed in black fur. They made a stunning pair, looking more like sisters than mother and daughter. Only Sasha's glowing red eyes and pale skin marked her as anything out of the ordinary.

"Ladies." Conryu bowed then grinned. "I trust you've been enjoying your time together?"

"It's been great," Anya said. "I'm starving, what's your mom fixing for dinner?"

"Turkey with all the trimmings, same as we have every year." Conryu held out his hand and when she took it he cast, "Cloak of Darkness."

With Anya protected from the energy of Hell, he opened a portal and they all stepped through. Cerberus was waiting to guide them home. Kai had to be close, but she didn't show herself. He'd invited the ninja to join them, but she claimed not to like crowds and begged off. She probably wanted to keep an eye on him from the borderland. As if Christmas dinner was some sort of military operation that might end with him in combat fighting for his life.

It didn't take long for them to reach the edge of Mrs. Kane's wards. After last summer she'd given him a special rune stone that allowed him to enter and exit the building without smashing holes in her protective spells. Speaking of which…

"I almost forgot." He dug a pair of engraved bronze rings out of his pocket and handed one to Talon and the other to Sasha. "These'll protect you from the effects of the wards around my apartment building. Mrs. Kane didn't want to alter them to allow in undead since not everyone is as friendly and well-mannered as you guys."

"Perfectly reasonable." Talon slipped the ring on.

When Sasha had hers in place, Conryu opened another portal into his living room and they stepped out.

Conryu's mouth watered as the aroma of roasting turkey mingled with the spicy-sweet scent of the surprise dessert.

"Hi, Mom."

His mother nearly leapt out of her shoes when he spoke. She was busy stirring six pots on the stove while Kelsie finished setting the table. "How many times have I told you to make a noise when you open one of those things?"

"Once, and I told you I don't know how to do that. Prime, do you know how to do that?"

"No, Master. I'm not certain it's possible."

"There you go, straight from the scholomantic's mouth."

Mom growled at them, but she didn't mean it. The little wrinkle between her eyes said so.

Anya gasped. "That smell. Is it…?"

Conryu grinned and helped her off with her coat. "Baked apples. I asked Sasha for the recipe so we could surprise you."

She hugged him then her mother. "I can't wait."

Mom waved at the dining room where a pair of tables had been shoved together to make room for everyone. "Have a seat. We'll be ready in fifteen minutes. Sho!"

His father emerged from the bedroom and bowed to his guests. "Welcome to our home. Please make yourselves comfortable."

He'd changed into his master's uniform, black pants and a white robe marked with a yin yang symbol on the back. Dad seldom wore it, so Mom must have insisted.

Talon, Sasha, and Anya had barely settled in when someone knocked. That had to be Maria and her parents.

He went to the door and sure enough there they were. Maria looked stunning in a black dress with her hair done up in some fancy style held together with black lacquered sticks. It showed off her slim, pale neck to excellent effect. Hopefully Talon didn't get any ideas. Conryu swore she got more beautiful every time he saw her.

He motioned them in and Mr. Kane made a beeline for Talon.

"He's been so excited ever since I told him we were having dinner with a VIP," Maria said. She took his arm and they walked to the table together.

Mr. Kane was shaking Talon's hand. "It's a great honor to have a head of state such as yourself joining us to celebrate the season. I hope this can be the beginning of new relations between our countries."

Talon smiled. "I wonder if the rest of your government will be equally enthusiastic to be associated with a vampire. It's been my experience that most humans find our company uncomfortable."

"There might be a few narrow-minded bureaucrats, they're unavoidable, but I believe most of my superiors are open to the possibility."

"Enough politics," Mom said. "Dinner's ready."

Dad brought the turkey over and started carving. Mom dished up the sides and placed them on the table. Now the moment of truth. She filled two goblets and put one in front of Talon and the other in front of Sasha.

"What is this?" Talon asked.

"Turkey blood, warmed and strained." Mom let out a nervous laugh. "You should have seen the look the butcher gave me when I asked for it. I said I was making turkey blood sausage. I hope it's to your taste."

Talon took a sip and everyone fell silent. His eyes went wide. "This is delightful. You know, in seventeen hundred years I've never thought to try the blood of a bird. It's very light, though there's also a hint of something else."

"Sage," Mom said. She sat beside Dad at the head of the table while Kelsie took the seat beside Conryu. "It goes really nicely with poultry so I sprinkled just a bit in the pot."

"It tastes fantastic. When Conryu mentioned you made a special dish for us, I never imagined something so unique. Please accept my most sincere thanks."

Mom blushed a little and started passing the bowls around to cover it. Who'd have imagined his mother hitting it off with a vampire? Now if he could just convince her to like Prime a little better.

* * *

Conryu sighed and finished off the last of his baked apple. Anya was right, they were delicious. He doubted he could eat another bite. All around the table everyone seemed to share his opinion, even the vampires, and they'd only had a glass of blood each. They must have small stomachs.

Kelsie yawned and that started a chain reaction. Nothing like a big meal to make you sleepy. Talon rose and so did Sasha.

"We should be getting back," Talon said. "Thank you again for a wonderful meal. I can't remember the last time I did something like this."

Everyone else stood to say goodbye. "We'll have to do this again sometime," Mom said. "It's probably not polite to say this, but you hear the stories and well, I'm glad I got to meet a real vampire."

Dad just bowed. Mr. Kane gave Talon's hand another enthusiastic shake and blathered on about relations. Talon accepted the attention with a good deal more patience than Conryu would have.

He turned to Anya. "Are you going with your mom, or are you staying here with us?"

"I'll stay. Mom says it wouldn't be thoughtful to ask you to make another trip to pick me up. We only have a couple days before school starts."

"Cool. You and Kelsie can decide who gets the couch and who gets the air mattress." Conryu twisted off the last leg of the turkey. He doubted Cerberus got hungry, but then again he might like a treat. He'd fix Kai something tonight when everyone was asleep.

Damn it. He'd almost forgotten. Conryu made a quick run to his room and collected a package wrapped in black paper, not exactly festive, but the Dark Lady would probably appreciate it.

"Are we ready?" he asked.

Talon disengaged from Mr. Kane. "We are."

Conryu opened the portal and led the way through. Cerberus appeared almost at once. Conryu tossed the turkey leg up and the center head snapped it out of the air. It barely made a bite for the huge hound, but Cerberus gave his happy bark anyway.

"It was a pleasure to meet your family," Talon said. "Though Orin came on a bit strong."

"Well, Mr. Kane doesn't get to Central very often, so he misses out on a lot of meet and greets with important folks. He says it like it's a bad thing. I'm sure he enjoyed having you all to himself."

They followed Cerberus to the Land of the Night Princes. Before he opened a portal for them Sasha said, "I'm glad Anya found a friend like you, someone she can trust. We can't offer her much in the way of a family, so thank you for sharing yours."

"My pleasure. She's great to hang out with. So what do you say, Easter dinner? Maybe Mom can find you some rabbit blood."

They shared a laugh.

Conryu opened a portal. "See you next Sunday."

Talon nodded, but before the vampires had a chance to enter the real world Kai appeared. "You almost forgot, Chosen." She held out a box sealed with a ribbon.

Conryu slapped his forehead. "Thanks, Kai."

He took the package and handed it to Talon. "Merry Christmas."

Talon looked from the box and back to him. "What's this?"

"Open it."

Talon sliced the ribbon with a razor-sharp nail and took off the lid. He reached in and pulled out the Solar Orb. "Why?"

"I figured no one would do a better job protecting it than you and this way you won't worry about where it is."

"Won't your superiors be upset with you for giving away something so valuable?"

"I'm sure they would've been, if I told anyone I had it. I considered giving it to you at once, but I wanted to try to figure out how it worked. After three months I still don't have a clue. Rather than keep it as the world's most valuable paper-weight, I figured I'd let you hang on to it."

"Thank you. Having this device in hand takes a weight off my mind, even if there are two more out in the world."

"Two that we know of," Prime said. "Who can say how many more might be hiding in still-unexplored elf ruins."

"You certainly have a way of killing the moment, Prime. Talon, Sasha, see you later."

The vampires left Hell and when he'd closed the portal he called, "Dark Lady."

One more present to deliver then he could go home and have a nice long nap. While they waited for his agent to arrive Kai fiddled with the silver ring on her right ring finger. It was a minor magical item that would allow her to sense if he was injured or in trouble. Since she kept a constant watch over him, it probably wasn't necessary, but he wanted to try making a magic item and this was the simplest one he could find in the library. St. Seraphim had checked and deemed it an acceptable first effort.

"Is it uncomfortable? The enchantment should adjust the size to fit you perfectly."

"It fits fine, Chosen, it's just that no one has given me a gift, unless you count my sword, since I joined the Daughters of The Reaper. When I was assigned to serve as your protector, I never imagined we might become friends."

Conryu grinned. "I'd rather have a friend watching my back than someone doing a job."

He cocked his head. The Dark Lady was approaching. He spotted her a moment later. Soon the glowing dot resolved itself into her stunning figure.

The Dark Lady stopped and floated before him. "You summoned me, Master? Has something happened?"

"Nothing important." He held out the box. "I wanted to give you your Christmas present."

She laughed and clapped her hands. "A gift! How delightful. You know, Master, wizards seldom give presents to their demonic servants."

"I informed him of that," Prime said. "But he insisted on buying you something anyway."

"Are you going to open it or not?" Conryu asked.

"I certainly am." The Dark Lady took the box and tore it open. She gasped. "Master, they're beautiful."

She tossed the box aside and displayed a pair of black thigh-high leather boots with five-inch heels. While she pulled them on he said, "I can't take all the credit. My girlfriend helped me pick them out. I had to guess on the size, but being a demon I figured you could always shape shift to make them fit."

She zipped up the side of the second boot and extended a flawless leg to show them off. "They're perfect, thank you. I shall treasure them. The first gift ever given to me."

"No one's ever given you a gift?" Conryu hardly believed the beautiful demon had never received a present.

"Displaying that sort of sentimentality isn't wise in Hell, Master," Prime said. "It could be seen as a sign of weakness."

"That's ridiculous. We're a team and doing something nice for a teammate isn't a sign of weakness. I depend on you guys and I want you to know I appreciate your efforts on my behalf."

The Dark Lady darted in and kissed his cheek. "You are the best master ever."

Conryu grinned. That was more like it.

* * *

Since he'd traveled through Hell, Conryu was home again less than a minute after he left. When he emerged in the living room, his mother had fallen fast asleep in the recliner. Maria, Anya, and Kelsie were cleaning up while Mr. and Mrs. Kane sat chatting with his father. Mr. Kane spotted him first and hopped to his feet.

He opened his mouth to speak, but Mrs. Kane grabbed his arm, pointed at Mom, and put a finger to her lips. He nodded and motioned toward the apartment door.

Conryu's over-full stomach did a somersault. He didn't even know what Mr. Kane wanted yet, but whatever it was it had to be dangerous at worst and a pain in the ass at best. He hoped for the latter as he'd had his fill of life-threatening situations, at least for a few months.

Mr. Kane reached the door first and opened it for him. When they were outside he said, "I trust you got our special guests home safely."

"Yeah, no problem. So what does the Department need now?"

He winced. "You assume just because I asked to talk to you I want something?"

Conryu nodded. From one of the other apartments came the muted sound of Jingle Bells.

"It isn't dangerous this time, I swear."

"Uh-huh."

"You know tryouts for the Four Nations Tournament team are coming up, right?"

Conryu didn't like where this was going. "Yeah."

"The Department would like you to try out. You're eligible this year, though a sophomore hasn't made the team in a long time."

For a moment Conryu wished his hair was longer so he could pull it out. Of all the things he didn't want to do, competing in a televised magic competition ranked pretty high on the list. He wanted to be less famous, not more.

"I'll pass. I'm sure there are plenty of seniors who will be happy to join the team."

Mr. Kane rubbed the bridge of his nose. "Have you watched the games lately?"

"No. Last time I tried, lunatics with knives and hammers interrupted me."

"Well, I'll sum things up for you. Our teams have been terrible. They've placed last two years running and ratings reflect that. Even two years ago when Heather James, our most popular player in decades, was still on the team, ratings were falling. The only way things are going to turn around is if we do something drastic."

"As in having the only male wizard on the team?"

"Exactly." Mr. Kane paced as he got into his pitch. "Not only will your power give us an excellent chance of winning, but you're interesting. People are curious about you. The fact that you refuse to have anything to do with the press only makes you more intriguing. With you on the team I guarantee a five-point increase at least."

"I appreciate the vote of confidence, but team sports aren't my thing." Conryu took a step toward the apartment door then turned back. "Why does the Department care about ratings anyway?"

Mr. Kane refused to meet his gaze, never a good sign. "We get a portion of our research budget from licensing revenue the networks pay us. It works on a sliding scale based on ratings. The better the ratings the more money we get. We haven't exactly been getting rich lately. R&D is on my ass to turn things around."

"Look, I've been a pretty good sport about helping you guys out, haven't I? I like to think I've done my part the past year and a half. Now I want a little peace and quiet. No tv cameras, no reporters, no dragons or demons—except Prime and the others that work for me. I feel like I've earned a semester of leisure."

"You have, ten times over. Maybe you could just think about it? Tryouts aren't for another ten days. You might change your mind. You'd really be saving my bacon, Conryu."

Mr. Kane gave him a much less attractive version of Maria's patented sad puppy face. On a grown man it just looked pathetic.

"No promises, but I will give it some thought."

Mr. Kane beamed like he'd already said yes. "I knew I could count on you, Conryu."

Why did Conryu feel like a cartoon character with "sucker" stamped on his forehead?

2

BACK AT SCHOOL

C onryu made his way up to the wind magic floor to meet Dean Blane. He had a class with her this morning and was curious to find out what she had planned. Whatever she intended for the second half of the year, it had to be better than getting nagged about the tryouts.

In the two days since Mr. Kane had asked him to try out for the team, Maria's father had checked in twice to see if he'd changed his mind. Conryu almost gave in the second time just to get some peace. The only thing that stopped him was the fear that if he didn't put his foot down the Department would keep running over him.

He'd left the cafeteria early to avoid the girls in the other classes. Not that they were unpleasant, but they all stared at him as he passed. None of them seemed aware they were doing it, it was more of a reflex. Conryu liked to avoid dealing with them when possible.

Over winter break, whoever handled remodeling at the school had removed the door connecting his room to Anya's.

She had moved up to the earth magic floor, with the others that shared her alignment. Anya had been quick to agree when Dean Blane suggested the move which surprised him and thrilled Maria. She claimed she trusted him, but why keep temptation so close at hand?

When he reached the classroom where Dean Blane said to meet her he found it empty. Guess he'd arrived too early. He took a chair in the front row, leaned back, and put his feet on the table. Prime flew beside him.

"What do you think?" Conryu asked. "Should I try out or not?"

"You clearly don't want to," Prime said. "I can feel it through our link. I can also tell you're conflicted by your desire to help someone you consider a friend. That's your problem. You're too worried about others. Demons simply satisfy their whims and damn the consequences."

"I'm aware of my mental failings, thank you. I was asking for your opinion."

"I couldn't care less, Master."

Conryu groaned and shook his head. "Thanks, pal. You're a huge help."

The door opened and Dean Blane entered. "You're here bright and early. Eager to get started?"

"Yeah, what are we doing?"

"Since it's too cold to play outside, we're going to summon spirits. Wind spirits as a matter of fact. I'm curious to see how they react to you. We know your alignment gives you a boost when casting wind spells, so it'll be interesting to see if they treat you as a fully wind-aligned wizard or something else."

"What else could they treat me as?"

She grinned. "I have no idea. That's what makes this so interesting."

Dean Blane went up to the chalkboard and drew a spell circle. He didn't recognize any of the little squiggles so Conryu assumed they were written in the language of wind.

Come to think of it… "How am I supposed to talk to them when I only know about ten words of their language?"

"Oh, yeah, I forgot." She dug a scroll out of her robe and tossed it to him. "Memorize then cast that spell."

Conryu unrolled the scroll. "This looks like St. Seraphim's handwriting."

"It's a light magic spell that allows you to hear and speak any language. Almost every wizard knows it. It's super handy when dealing with spirits not from your alignment, or humans that don't speak English for that matter."

"It's written in Angelic," Conryu said. "I can't read that very well either."

"Right. I keep forgetting you're just a sophomore. You can do so much it's easy to think you have all the knowledge of an experienced wizard. Place your index fingers at your temple and repeat after me: Understanding is the true path to peace, Perfect Translation."

He repeated the spell, but didn't notice anything different afterward. "Did it work?"

"You tell me. Can you understand what I'm saying?"

"Yeah."

"Then since I'm speaking in the language of wind, I'd say it worked. Now copy the spell circle and let's summon a pixie."

* * *

"I think you should try out for the team."

Conryu could only stare at Mrs. Umbra. Of all the people at school that he thought might want him to join, she never even crossed his mind. After lunch he'd gone to her office for dark magic class hoping they'd try summoning a demon. It had only taken him two tries to get a pixie with Dean Blane that morning and he was feeling lucky.

"Say what?"

"Joining the school team will be good for you. Working one on one will add spells to your repertoire quickly, but being part of a team will help you figure out how best to use them in combination with wizards of other alignments. That's a useful skill that we don't spend nearly enough time on."

Conryu settled into his usual chair. "Oh, and here I thought you were worried about the Department's R&D budget. Seriously though, do you think it'll really make much difference?"

She nodded and leaned over her desk so their noses were almost touching. "Teamwork is vital for a wizard, even one as powerful as you. When I served on the southern border, being able to work as a seamless unit saved the lives of my team more than once. Better for you if you learn it in a safe environment. The tournament's all about bragging rights and showing off, but that doesn't make the lessons any less valuable."

"I'd be more open to it if I could avoid the press. The problem is they want to use me as the star attraction. It makes me feel like a sideshow freak for people to stop and stare at."

Mrs. Umbra gave a dismissive wave of the Death Stick. "Bah! Forget about that foolishness. Tell them what they want to hear and move on. Try being boring. That seems to do wonders to keep the press away, or you can fry their cameras with dark magic."

Conryu grinned. He knew how to do that. "I'll consider it. Maybe I won't even make the team."

She barked a laugh. "The dark magic user's main job is dispelling the opposing team's spells. I can say with absolute confidence there's no one at this school better at Dispel than you and I include teachers in that assessment."

"I appreciate your confidence in me. Now, what are we studying this semester?"

"Summoning. It's time you learned how to bring a demon to this world and keep it under control."

He'd guessed right, awesome. "Should we start with Cerberus or the Dark Lady?"

"Are you crazy? We're starting with an imp and then perhaps a normal hell hound. You need way more experience before you try to summon anything as powerful as Cerberus."

That was disappointing, but he shouldn't have been surprised considering all the warnings he'd gotten about not bringing the demon dog to their reality. A regular hell hound might still be interesting. If nothing else at least he spoke the language this time.

* * *

Lady Tiger hated the Blessed Kingdom. The zealots made her skin crawl. It didn't help that they'd all happily burn her at the stake if they learned she was a wizard. So she found herself pacing in an empty, snow-filled clearing two hundred miles from the nearest civilization waiting for an agent of the Archbishop to meet her.

The glare from the midday sun nearly blinded her. The sooner she could leave this wretched place the better. All around the clearing, bare, skeletal trees thrust their thin black limbs toward the sky. A pair of ravens perched in one of the trees, their shiny black eyes searching for a meal.

At least her fire aura kept the cold from being a bother, though she still pulled her fur-lined cloak tight about her in case some hunter should see her standing untroubled by the chill and assume she was an evil spirit in need of cleansing. Then she'd have to kill him and that wouldn't make a good impression on her hosts. Not that she cared what they thought of her, but she wanted to strike a bargain and anything that impeded her mission had to be avoided.

The snow crunched to her left and she spun to find a man in black facing her at the edge of the woods. The ravens took off with a chorus of caws. Now completely alone with the stranger, she took a moment to study him.

Nothing stood out beyond the white collar of his black uniform. He had a medium build, medium height, and thinning hair. If she'd seen a more ordinary man she couldn't recall it. No doubt that ordinariness served him well as a secret agent of the church.

He stepped out into the clearing. "You would be Lady Tiger."

"Father Salvador. We meet at last."

"Indeed, though I shall require purification after this conversation."

Lady Tiger knew what he meant. Dealing with the self-righteous priests always left her feeling dirty, too. "Has His Holiness come to a decision?"

"The Archbishop has agreed to accept your aid. Though it pains him to rely on heathen wizards, the Kingdom's interference in our holy work must not go unanswered. Their meddling cost us control of France and they will suffer for it."

"He approves of the timing as well?" Lady Tiger asked.

The priest flashed a humorless smile. "He does. In fact, he thought the idea of striking during a gathering of the damned showed inspiration. God truly works in mysterious ways."

"My ship will wait for your first load of infiltrators one

week hence fifty miles off the coast. The window for infiltration only opens once every twenty days, so we must take full advantage."

"We've chosen our most devout warriors, all of them prepared to die for the cause." Father Salvador tapped his chin. "I have one question. Why would a wizard help her mortal enemies? Under different circumstances I would dance at your pyre."

"Under different circumstances I would burn the skin from your body and leave you to die in screaming agony. Suffice it to say having you in the Kingdom wreaking havoc during the tournament suits my purposes. I'll see your people delivered. Just make sure they do their part."

"Oh, they will. For God's glory."

Lady Tiger nodded. Ignorant cretin. She would take great pleasure in sacrificing these fools for Morgana's freedom.

* * *

Conryu stared at the ceiling in his room and tried to clear his mind. It was Saturday evening and he'd just finished a week of summoning low-level spirits from every element. He'd even succeeded with light magic, which seemed to annoy Prime no end. The scholomantic was pouting in his place on Conryu's table.

Not that he blamed Prime; that little angelic hummingbird thing he'd called was adorable with its rainbow wings and eyes like gems. It licked his cheek and buzzed all around him. It had paused by his sore right shoulder and moments later the pain vanished. St. Seraphim explained that the glitter sprite healed any damage it found on its summoner. It was one of the few ways a wizard could heal their own wounds.

Which explained why she'd wanted him to learn to summon it.

While summoning came as naturally to him as all the other magic he'd tried, keeping constant track of what the spirits were doing wore him out mentally more than a regular spell did. When he'd mentioned that to Dean Blane she assured him that once he mastered the basics, they could teach him how to weave control parameters into the summoning spell so he wouldn't have to focus every second.

Now he needed to decide what to do about tryouts tomorrow. He'd been debating all week and Maria hadn't been much help. On the one hand she wanted him to help out her dad, and on the other she didn't want him to let the Department use him. She ended up saying whatever he decided was okay with her.

Prime flew up off the desk. "Someone's coming, Master."

Conryu frowned and sat up on his bed. Prime knew the other students' and teachers' life forces by now. If he was reacting it had to be a stranger, but who would be visiting him here of all places?

Whoever it was knocked and he got up to answer it, the words of a spell at the front of his mind. He opened the door and his jaw dropped.

The woman in the hall had long blond hair, bright blue eyes, and a perfect smile. A tight blue top hugged her curves and left her flat midriff bare. Her black skirt ended at mid-thigh.

She held out a hand. "I'm Heather James. It's a pleasure to meet you at last, Mr. Koda."

Conryu closed his mouth and gave her hand a gentle shake. "Hi."

"Um, can I come in or do you want to talk out in the hall?"

He gave his head a little shake. "Yeah, come on in. Sorry, but I wasn't expecting to find a celebrity on my doorstep."

"It's okay." She brushed against him as she entered sending a shiver down his spine. "I get that reaction a lot. I see they haven't upgraded the dorms since I graduated."

She sat in his chair and crossed her legs, forcing the hem of her skirt up a little higher. Whether it was intentional or not, the effect was remarkable.

Conryu wasn't sure what to do. Standing up and staring down at her would be rude, but he only had the one chair. Somehow even approaching the bed with her in his room seemed wrong. Finally, he perched on the edge of the mattress.

"I bet you're wondering why I'm here."

He nodded. "The question crossed my mind. I thought you were off getting your picture taken in exotic locations."

"I was, but when the Department called and said they needed my help, I couldn't say no."

"Yeah, they seem to have me on speed dial too." Now that the initial shock had worn off, Conryu started getting his bearings. "What did they want you to do?"

"I'm going to be the assistant coach for the Academy team this year."

Wow, they were really going all out to improve ratings. "Congratulations. Was there something you wanted from me?"

"Just to make sure you're trying out tomorrow. I didn't leave a white sand beach and eighty-degree water to join a losing effort."

"I hadn't decided. The truth is I'm not much into team sports."

"Are you into money? If you join up and play your cards right, I guarantee you a multimillion-dollar endorsement deal if the team wins. My final year we came in last and I still got a three-million-dollar package from the modeling agency. Think what I'll command if I help coach the team to a championship."

Her decision to leave the beach made a good deal more sense now. He sighed. An endorsement deal didn't interest him. A little money in the bank wouldn't be a bad thing, but the idea of going on tv or filming a commercial left him sick.

Oh, what the hell. He'd be helping Mr. Kane out of a tough spot, this time without putting his life on the line. Not to mention Jonny would lose his mind when Conryu told him he was hanging out with Heather James. Hopefully, Maria wouldn't have a similar reaction.

"Alright, I'll be there. I'm still only a sophomore so some senior might beat me out."

Her smile took his breath away. "I'd bet my Porsche you make it without breaking a sweat. I've read the stories about what you did in Sentinel City. Compared to that, tryouts are a cinch."

3

TRYOUTS

Sunday midmorning arrived and the glare off the snow forced Conryu to squint as he stepped out of the dorm. Hardly a cloud floated through the sky and a cold wind swirled off the frozen lake. Fire Aura kept him comfortable in his black robe.

Tryouts were due to start in a little while. He didn't want to arrive too early as waiting around in the cold didn't appeal to him, even if he couldn't feel it. After his evening chat with Heather last night he'd had an awful time getting to sleep. It struck him as manipulation to send the woman most people considered the most beautiful in the world to ask him to join up. Just having her standing on the sidelines should be good for a point of improved ratings. He'd watch for her legs alone.

"Conryu."

He glanced up at Crystal as the earth magic senior joined him on the steps. "Hey, you trying out?"

She nodded. "I barely missed making the team last year and

the girl that beat me graduated so I think I've got a good chance. What about you?"

"Yeah, everyone on the Department payroll seems to want me to. It'll be interesting to see how I stack up against the dark magic seniors."

Prime snorted. "I can tell you exactly how you stack up against a bunch of students who've never been in real combat in their sheltered lives. They should offer you the position outright if they want you to join so bad."

"That wouldn't be fair," Conryu said. "I need to earn my spot, the same as everyone else."

He knew he was supposed to say that, but he suspected Prime's was the more honest assessment. Still, maybe he'd be surprised.

"Want to walk down together?" Conryu asked.

"Sure. I hope we both make it. It'll be fun to be on a team together again."

Conryu led the way down a well-worn path to the lake. "If Sonja was here to represent fire, it would be just like the golem club only with a few extras. Speaking of our fearless leader, have you talked to her?"

"All the time. She's having a blast at her job. They're working on some top-secret government project so she can't give me any details."

"That's good. Sonja seemed so conflicted last year. I'm glad she's settled in."

Crystal nodded. "We should invite her to join us in London, assuming we're on the team. It'll be like a reunion."

"I'm down with that."

More girls in robes of all colors joined them as they moved closer to the lake. A small crowd had already gathered and two figures stood off by themselves closer to the shore.

"That's weird," Crystal said. "There's usually just one coach. I wonder who the extra is?"

Conryu knew exactly who it was, but he figured they were going to make a big deal out of announcing her so he didn't want to spoil the surprise. "We'll find out soon enough I expect."

They merged with the crowd already waiting and settled in. Crystal stood up on her tiptoes and squinted. "Is that Heather James? It sure looks like her."

"I can't see," Conryu said. It was the truth, even if not the whole truth.

Stragglers continued to arrive over the next ten minutes. When a full minute passed with no one else showing up, a stern woman with short hair wearing a gray, Department-issue robe stepped forward.

"My name is Melisandra Chort." She had a deep, almost masculine voice. "You will address me as Coach Chort or just Coach. We are here today to find out which of you has what it takes to represent the Alliance at this year's tournament. I see some familiar faces. Just because you made the team last year doesn't guarantee you a spot this year."

She locked eyes with Conryu. "I don't care how famous you are or what you've done to make you think you deserve a spot on my team. You can either do the job or you can't. You may have noticed we have a special guest today. This is Heather James, a former team captain. She will serve as my assistant coach. She has real-world experience. I suggest you take advantage of it."

Heather moved up closer to Coach Chort. She'd traded her sexy outfit from last night for a blue-green water wizard's robe. "I'm looking forward to working with this year's team.

We've had a rough run of luck, but this year I'm sure we'll turn things around."

She flashed a brilliant smile and winked at Conryu.

"Alright," Coach Chort said. "Let's get the trials underway."

* * *

Coach Chort ordered everyone to line up by element. Conryu wished Crystal a final good luck and moved to the far right-hand side of the gathering. Four girls in black robes eyed him the way he'd look at a dead rat on the kitchen floor. He didn't recognize any of them and assumed they were seniors. None of them had a familiar which didn't surprise him. Other than wind wizards, most everyone considered them a liability. Then again, most wizards didn't have a familiar as awesome as Prime.

When everyone had finished sorting themselves out, Coach Chort said, "Alright, we'll start with light magic. This isn't actual combat, so the need for healing should be minimal. What we'll be testing for is your ability to integrate with other elements. Heather."

Heather wove her hands in a circular motion and chanted. A sphere of water formed and floated in the air. Coach Chort cast a spell of her own, encasing the sphere in earth.

"Now, I want each light wizard to cast Elemental Fusion. If you don't know it, you can leave now. Whoever does the best job merging the separate spells into one gets the job."

Conryu watched as one white-robed girl after another cast the same spell. It made the earth-and-water globe glow to varying degrees. If it did anything else, he couldn't tell.

When they'd finished, Heather and Coach Chort released their spells. The coach pointed at the third girl who'd cast.

"Congratulations, your fusion functioned at over eighty percent, the best by fifteen percent. You make the team."

The girl thrust her fists into the air. "Yes!"

The other light magic users grumbled and started toward the dorm.

"Okay, now water," Coach Chort said. "We'll be conjuring water serpents, biggest one wins."

The result of the test was as simple as it was obvious. The winning girl's serpent was half again as tall as the next strongest person's. It struck Conryu as the fire wizards lined up that it would be simpler just to go through the applicants' test results and choose the ones with the strongest magical potential.

"Raw power doesn't always indicate who's the better wizard," Prime said. "Skill also enters into it. A weaker wizard with better control of her energy flow might get a superior result. That's why they're doing the tests, or so I assume."

Conryu was just starting to think maybe he wouldn't get stuck on the team when Prime added, "That's assuming the competing wizards are close in overall power. When you're five times stronger than your competition, efficiency becomes much less of an issue."

So much for that hope. The fire wizards had finished their testing and Crystal and the other earth wizards took their places center stage.

"The earth wizard is probably the most important piece of the team," Coach Chort said. "The ability to create physical obstacles to the opposing team is key in the group melee. Each of you is going to cast Stone Behemoth. In addition to its offensive potential, the spell can serve as a mobile wall between you and those trying to blast you. You're going to pair off and battle. Durability is every bit as important as size in this circumstance."

Only four earth wizards had showed up to try out so it wouldn't take long to get them sorted out. Crystal and her opponent went first. The stone giants they summoned each stood about ten feet tall and half that wide. Their features were blunt and crude, but basically recognizable.

The two behemoths came together with a crash. Shoulder to shoulder, hands locked, they pushed, churning up the snow and sending clods of frozen earth flying.

Crystal's creature pulled back first before launching a punch that sent the opposing monster's head flying out over the lake. Conryu thought that would be the end of it, but since the giants were nothing but mounds of earth, the lack of a head didn't bother them.

The giants traded blows until only a gasping Crystal's behemoth remained standing, albeit with three head-sized holes smashed in its chest. Once it had collapsed into a pile of dirt and stone, the second pair had their match. The spells produced foes of similar size, but one of the girls lacked stamina and soon collapsed in an unconscious heap.

When Crystal faced up to her second opponent, it was clear the other girl was fresher. That was proven out when Crystal's behemoth appeared at only eight feet high. The grin on Crystal's opponent said she knew she had the upper hand.

Two heavy blows drove the head of Crystal's behemoth down into its chest. She was losing and losing ugly.

"Go for its legs!" Conryu shouted.

Crystal's behemoth ducked an incoming punch and leapt at the legs of its opponent. Instead of tackling it, the heavy impact smashed both legs to bits and sent the upper portion crashing to the ground.

A few heavy blows to the fallen creature ended the match with Crystal as the winner.

Conryu grinned, but the other girls all glared at him. If he wasn't supposed to help, someone should have said something. This was a team competition after all.

When the coach didn't complain, Crystal staggered over and hugged him. "Thanks. I never would have thought of going low."

"Since your creature was shorter, it made sense. I'm glad it worked. This wouldn't be nearly as much fun if you didn't make the team."

"Maybe you'll be the one that doesn't make the team," one of the dark magic wizards snarled at him.

Conryu shrugged. "Maybe."

The wind test came next. They were tasked to find an object hidden on the island and retrieve it using a summoned spirit. Whoever succeeded won the test.

Ten minutes later a scroll cylinder came zipping across the lake and landed in the hand of one of the few juniors trying out for the team. The senior wind wizards grumbled, but no one complained too loud.

"Last but not least comes dark magic," Coach Chort said. "Your primary task will be using Dispel against our opponents' spells. To that end we'll be testing the power of your castings. Don't hold back as I need an accurate idea of what you can do. Heather."

Heather raised her hands and summoned a water dragon in the sky above the lake. Conryu remembered that spell from the last tournament he watched, it provided the basis of the combined conjuring from the first round.

The coach pointed at one of the seniors. "You first."

She took a couple steps closer to the water's edge and put her hands together. "Darkness dispels everything!"

The dark sphere slammed into the dragon and exploded. Dark magic washed over the construct and sent it splashing down into the lake.

"Ha!" The dark wizard pumped her fist. "Beat that."

Heather summoned the dragon three more times, but none of the other girls fully dispelled it. The coach turned her hard gaze on Conryu. "Let's see what you got, boy."

Heather repaired the damage to her construct and gave him a smile of encouragement. "I'm going to try something different," Conryu said.

"I'm not sure this is a good idea, Master. Trying a new spell during such an important test might not be wise."

"Yeah, but I'm going to do it anyway." Conryu put his hands together and chanted. "Darkness dispels everything."

He chanted it over and over, compressing the magic with each casting like he did with Focused Dispel. Black lightning flicked out as the power built. When he couldn't contain it a second more Conryu hurled the baseball-sized sphere of dark energy at the dragon. It punched through, leaving a small hole in its side.

The dark wizards laughed.

"Is that the best you can do?" the girl who'd dispelled the dragon first asked.

Conryu grinned and snapped his fingers, releasing the energy stored in the sphere.

A pillar of inky black power exploded out and up, consuming the dragon and blocking out the sun for a second. When the mini eclipse passed he said, "Yeah, that's about the best I can do."

Everyone stared in silence until Coach Chort said, "Congratulations, Conryu. You made the team. Everyone that didn't make the cut is excused. The rest of you line up."

Crystal moved to stand beside him. "That was awesome."

"Thanks. I'd been wanting to try that variation of the spell for a little while now, but I didn't know when I'd get the chance."

Heather took her place beside the coach. A light sheen of sweat covered her face. She probably hadn't cast that many spells in a row for a while.

"Well, you did it," Coach Chort said. "But making the team is the easy part. Now you need to learn to fight together as a cohesive unit. We'll be working on that for the next twenty Sundays. I've seen what you can do and I say with confidence that you're the strongest group we've had in a decade. If you're willing to work hard, we have a real chance of winning this year. The rest of the day is yours. Training begins next Sunday. Dismissed."

Conryu gave a little shake of his head. Dismissed? She sounded more like a drill sergeant than a coach. He still didn't know how to feel about making the team, but he'd done it and that meant he had to give it everything he had.

"Want to get lunch?" Crystal asked.

"Sure. I've got to tell Maria and the others the good news."

"That you made the team or that Heather James is the assistant coach?" Prime asked.

"Stop reading my mind."

Crystal and Conryu had barely left the lakeshore when Heather came running up to join them. The assistant coach beamed at them. "Congratulations, both of you. You both gave impressive displays."

"Thanks," Crystal said. "I see you haven't lost your touch either."

Heather cracked her knuckles. "I try to keep in practice. Some models travel on a private plane, I like going by portal. Saves all kinds of time. I wonder if you could give Conryu and I a moment alone?"

"Um, okay." Crystal lengthened her stride and started to pull away from them.

"I'll catch up to you in the cafeteria," Conryu called after her. "So what's up? I'm on the team like you and everyone else wanted."

"Yes, and I'm sure everyone at the Department will be thrilled. What we need to talk about is your style. Also, is that girl someone you're in a relationship with?"

"Not the kind of relationship you mean. We're friends. Now what's wrong with my style?"

"It's indifferent. When you were trying out, I got the feeling watching you that you didn't care one way or the other whether you made the team."

"I didn't, but rest assured I don't do anything halfway. I'm on the team now and I'll do my best to see that we win."

She shook her head. "You need to do more than that. We're the headliners. You need to show enthusiasm, some flare, get excited about the competition. For goodness' sake act like it matters to you."

"I'll work on that. If there's nothing else, I need to go."

She sighed. "No, that's all for now. See you next Sunday."

"Sure." Conryu left her on the path and hurried back to the dorm. What would be the best way to fake caring about the competition? He didn't know, but winning a few matches should take care of any complaints.

* * *

"You made the team? That's great!" Maria hugged him. "Dad'll be so relieved. They take the loss of revenue seriously."

"I know." Conryu sat beside her and across from Crystal.

Anya was nowhere to be found and Kelsie hadn't left cooking club yet. The pulled pork sandwich he got at the kitchen smelled great and his stomach growled in agreement. It had been a long morning and he was starving.

While he ate, Crystal picked up the conversation. "Did you know the Department was hiring Heather James to serve as assistant coach?"

Conryu couldn't see Maria's reaction, but the moment of silence spoke volumes. "Dad didn't mention it. Why would they do that? When Heather was team captain, they still came in last."

Conryu set his half-eaten sandwich down. "I doubt it had anything to do with her coaching ability. She's there to look good on camera and get attention. She's certainly got a knack for it."

"What did she want to talk to you about anyway?" Crystal asked.

"My attitude. She says I need to act more excited about competing."

"Representing the Alliance is an honor," Crystal said.

"That's a good line. You should use it when the reporters show up. As for me, I've had about all the honors I can take. At least this one isn't apt to be delivered posthumously." He ate a couple more bites, sighed, and looked up. "Sorry. I'm just a little bitter about the whole situation. When the bell rings I'll be ready."

The subject of conversation shifted quickly after his

outburst to everyone's apparent relief. Crystal and Maria chatted about their studies while he finished up.

When the food was gone Conryu got to his feet. "I'm going to head to the library. I want to do some research. See you guys later."

He left Maria and Crystal and marched over to the library. Why was he so annoyed? Guilting him into joining the team wasn't that big a deal. No one's life hung in the balance. The tournament served as a bit of mindless entertainment, a chance for wizards of the four allied nations to show what they could do. Win or lose, who cared?

More important matters required his attention.

The library covered several thousand square feet. Bookshelves filled most of it, with an occasional table thrown in for good measure. The librarian had Sunday off, just like everyone else. Students still had permission to do research, but they were on their own.

That suited Conryu perfectly.

"Are we alone, Prime?"

"Yes, Master. You're the only human in the library."

"Good. Kai?"

The ninja appeared, her makeshift satchel hanging from her shoulder. She started to speak, but Conryu raised a finger to silence her. Outside magic wasn't allowed on the Academy campus. He was betting that by having Kai bring the elf artifacts in via the borderland they wouldn't set off the alarms.

When two minutes passed and no teachers came running in to confiscate the items, he deemed his guess correct.

"What were you going to say?" Conryu asked.

"Only that I watched your display on the lakeshore this morning and found it most impressive."

"Thanks. In a real fight you rarely have time to build up

power like that. Let's get to work. I don't suppose you have any research experience?"

Kai bowed her head. "I'm sorry, Chosen. Our training was of a more martial nature."

"That's okay. We'll just have to muddle through the best we can. Let's start with that ruby ring."

She dug it out and handed it to him. It was a pretty bauble for sure. Pure gold with a shining red gem in the center. Indecipherable runes crawled along the band.

"You ever seen these markings before, pal?"

Prime flew in closer. "It's Elvish, but I'm not fluent in either reading or speaking the language. The only phrase I can make out is 'prince of flame.'"

"Well, that's not ominous at all. Let's see if we can find an Elvish-to-English dictionary. Kai, would you copy the runes in my notebook, please?"

She nodded and sat at the table.

Conryu and Prime made their way over to the catalogue. He went right to the E section and pulled out the drawer. The selection on elves was depressingly thin. Only six books with "elf" in the title and none of them covered translations.

"I guess if they were easy to identify elf artifacts wouldn't be so mysterious. You're a book, which one do you think we should start with?"

Prime grumbled in Infernal. "I'm a demon that happens to have the appearance of a book, not an actual book. That said, before my transformation it would be fair to say that I was as close to a scholar as demons got. I suppose we'd best start with the basics. I recommend *Elves and Their Culture*."

Conryu followed the card's directions and found the book. It was two inches thick and covered with dust. Apparently elves weren't an area of particular interest.

He flipped to the first page and grimaced. Huge paragraphs and tiny print, great. If he had trouble falling asleep, this should solve his problem. He could either try to read it or have the pixie drop it on his head.

"I don't suppose you can just absorb this and tell me what it says?"

"I'm sorry, Master. That ability is limited to the subject I was created to teach."

"So only books on dark magic?"

Prime flexed his cover. "Even I can hold only so much information. A limiting principle was necessary."

Terrific. Hopefully the book would at least tell him something about the artifacts.

* * *

Maria pushed the last of her lunch around her tray. She'd never seen Conryu so out of sorts. Did he really hate the idea of joining the team that much? If so, he should have just told her father outright that he wasn't doing it. Right, and the sun should decide to rise in the west.

She should have been mad at her father. He knew Conryu loved them like a second family and would do anything to help out. Being manipulated by someone you loved would put anyone out of sorts. Not to mention all the stress from helping the former witches find their families. No, she didn't blame him for wanting a little time to himself.

She should go talk to him, tell him she understood. The library was usually empty on Sunday, it would be a good place for them to talk.

She looked up from her plate and found Crystal gone. Talk about distracted, Maria hadn't even noticed her go. Oh, well.

It didn't take long to make the walk to the library. The silent rows of bookcases kind of gave her the creeps.

"This is so boring." Maria homed in on Conryu's voice.

"It's a scholarly treatise, Master, not a novel. Perhaps it gets more interesting later."

"It certainly couldn't get any less interesting."

She rounded a bookcase and found Conryu hunched over a book, his head held in both hands.

"Hi."

He flinched and spun to face her. "Hey, what's up?"

"You seemed so upset when you left I thought we should talk."

"Oh, yeah, sorry about that. I was feeling a little down. It's been a hectic year and a half and I'd hoped for a little relaxation."

"I know. If you really don't want to participate, why don't you just quit? Dad'll understand." She sat beside him and took his hands. "It's not worth the headache if you're going to be miserable."

He smiled. Not the cocky grin, but a genuine, almost sad smile.

"I appreciate that, but I've committed now and I refuse to let my teammates down. The tournament probably won't be anywhere near as bad as I expect. Who knows, I might have fun, except for dealing with the press of course."

"That's the spirit." She glanced at the book he was reading as well as the open notebook. A column of strange runes written in an unfamiliar hand covered most of the page. They looked vaguely familiar, like something she'd read in one of her mother's books. "Is that Elvish?"

"Yeah. There's a mystery I need to solve. I should have

asked you to help me in the first place, but I was afraid it might be dangerous."

Maria crinkled her brow as she frowned. What was he mucking about with now? "Well, I'm here. Why don't you tell me all about it?"

"Okay, if you're sure. First, I need to introduce you to someone. Kai."

Who was Kai? Maria had never heard the name before. From out of nowhere a girl in all black appeared, the hilt of a sword jutting up from behind her shoulder. She looked like a ninja straight out of the movies.

"Maria, meet Kai, my bodyguard. Apparently being marked by the Reaper gets you a ninja to watch your back. Kai saved me twice when I was helping the vampires."

The girl, Kai, bowed to Maria. "The Chosen speaks most highly of you. It's an honor to meet you."

Maria stared, first at Kai then at Conryu. "Chosen?"

"Chosen of Death. It's my official title to Kai and her fellow ninjas. It's a long story and doesn't have anything to do with what I'm researching. See, I found a few interesting items in the Dragon Czar's palace. Show her, Kai."

The ninja — god, even thinking it sounded insane — emptied a cloth container onto the table revealing fourteen glittering items. Maria blinked and tried to convince herself she was imagining things. When neither Kai nor the items vanished she shook her head.

"Please tell me you didn't bring magic items onto school grounds. That's against the rules. The teachers will find them. Say, why aren't they here now?"

"Kai can travel through the border of Hell. It allowed her to bypass the wards, at least I assume that's what happened. And these aren't just magic items, they're elf artifacts. I need to figure out what they do. Hence the research."

"Elf artifacts!"

Conryu clamped a hand over her mouth. "Shh. This is a library."

She nodded and he let go. "Do you have any idea how dangerous those are?"

"Some. Why do you think I didn't want to leave them lying around where anyone could find them?"

"You should give them to Dean Blane. She'll know what to do."

"Right. She'll turn them over to the Department and from there they'll end up in Malice's claws. Can you imagine that power-hungry woman with this many artifacts? I'll take my chances figuring them out on my own, thanks all the same."

He had a point, but she hated to admit it. Maria stared at the artifacts. In a million years she'd never imagined having the chance to even be in the same room as that many of the rare items, much less have a chance to research them. It was just too good an opportunity to pass up. Besides, if he tried to do it himself it would take forever.

"Alright, leave it to me. What do you know so far?"

He grinned and grabbed a ring set with a red gem. "This is the one I started with. There's a copy of the markings in my notebook. Prime recognized three words: prince of flame."

"Prince of flame most likely refers to an efreet. That'll give me another angle to pursue."

"Great. I'm sure you're more capable of doing research like this than I am. You can keep the notes we made." Conryu gathered the artifacts up and turned to give them to Kai.

"Leave the ring."

"I'm not sure that's a good idea."

"How am I supposed to research the artifact without having it in possession? Don't you trust me?"

"I trust you completely, but keeping the artifacts out of the human realm as much as possible is way safer. If you have the ring on you, one of the teachers will sense it just as sure as anything. Any time you want to look at it just let me know and we'll bring it out, but for now it's better if Kai holds on to them."

She knew he had a point, but to possess an elf artifact of her own, even if it wasn't really hers, would be incredible. It wasn't fair that he had fourteen of them.

"Fine. I'll work on translating the notes. But if I figure out how to use it, I get to activate the ring."

"Deal."

* * *

The gymnasium was empty on Sundays so it made a perfect place for the team to hold their first practice. It also had enchantments to protect the building from errant spells, so that helped as well. When Conryu arrived, the bleachers had been pushed back, leaving a space about one hundred by one hundred and fifty feet for them to use. Seemed plenty big to Conryu, but he had no idea what the coach had in mind for their first day of training.

Probably nothing too extreme. None of them had ever worked together unless you counted Conryu and Crystal building magical constructs and that wasn't exactly combat. He'd expected to arrive last, but it looked like he made it first. The only other person in the room was Coach Chort. She wore a perpetual frown that matched her wrinkled robe. What would it take to get the woman to smile? He tried to imagine it and failed. Her face would likely shatter.

"Mr. Koda," Coach Chort said. "Nice to see you showing a bit of enthusiasm. I hadn't expected you to arrive first."

He hadn't intended to arrive first, but better to accept the compliment. "Thanks, Coach. What are we working on today?"

"I'll tell you when the others get here, that way I won't have to repeat myself."

"Fair enough. What happened to last year's coach?" Conryu didn't know the woman's name, but he knew it wasn't this stern gargoyle.

"What do you think? After three years finishing in last place, the Department fired her and hired me to whip you lot into shape. I guarantee we won't be finishing last this year."

That was an overly bold prediction given that she had no idea what the others could do in a real fight. On the other hand, she probably couldn't do her job if she lacked confidence.

The light and fire wizards arrived in short order. He didn't remember their names, that wasn't a good sign. Crystal arrived next and he sighed in relief, finally someone that wasn't a total stranger. The wind and water wizards arrived last. Of Heather there was no sign.

No matter. Like she said, she was only there to get attention. Given her record as team captain, she didn't have much to offer in the way of winning advice anyway.

"Alright, everyone line up," Coach Chort said.

They stood shoulder to shoulder, with Conryu on the end beside Crystal. Their coach walked up and down the line inspecting them like they were soldiers newly arrived at boot camp. In a way maybe they were. Although having been mixed up in a real war, it was hard for him to take this competition too seriously.

Coach Chort finally stopped and stood facing them, hands clasped behind her back. "Today we have our first training session. Since the tournament committee doesn't give advanced notice as to which events will be held in any given year, we can't know for sure what you'll have to do. The only sure thing is that there will be one team casting event. They have it every year. So we'll focus on that. You girls will make a multi-layered construct then Mr. Koda will try to break it. If you can create something powerful enough to withstand his breaking, you'll be sure to win the competition."

The girls gathered in a circle and began casting. While they worked Prime flew down closer so only Conryu could hear what he said. "If those girls can create something that can withstand a Dispel like you used last week, I'll never chase the pixie again."

"Don't discount my teammates. They might surprise you."

Prime's snort conveyed what he thought of that suggestion most eloquently.

Fifteen minutes later a five-element dragon floated at the center of the circle. Coach Chort looked at Conryu. "Your turn. Take it easy though, okay? We don't want to damage the school's wards."

"Got it." He raised his hand and pointed at the dragon. "Break!"

A dark sphere streaked out, smashed into the construct, and blew it to pieces of glittering energy. To be on the safe side he'd used less than a third of his full power and that seemed excessive. Should he have held back more?

From the glares the girls shot his way the answer appeared to be yes. On the other hand, if their opponents went full strength it might take them by surprise. Better to anger his teammates than give them false expectations.

Coach Chort seemed to agree with him. "That was pathetic! Do it again and this time make it stronger. My niece could have shattered that dragon and she isn't even dark aligned."

The girls grumbled but started again. Coach Chort waved him over. Conryu joined her and raised an eyebrow.

"How close was that shot to your maximum?"

"A simple breaking like that uses about half as much power as my standard Dispel. I divided it in half again just to be sure I didn't break anything I didn't intend to."

She shook her head. "At least we're in good shape for the dark magic tests. Now I just need to get these others up to speed."

That was probably what passed for a compliment from the gruff coach. He'd take it, but if she planned to get the others up to his level, she had an impossible mission in front of her.

4

PRACTICE BATTLE

Conryu stood beside Crystal in the gym. The whole team had small packs in front of them. Why they had a day's worth of clothes Conryu had no idea. Coach Chort paced up and down the line doing her drill sergeant impression. Heather hadn't bothered to put in an appearance since the first day. Instead, she'd been on the road doing interviews to drum up interest in this year's tournament. Word was she'd done a good job, not that they'd know since the school didn't have any tvs.

After a month of training, Conryu and his teammates were learning to work together. Or he should say the others were learning to work together. As the dark magic user, Conryu couldn't combine his element with any of the others since all it did was cause their spells to fail. He spent most of his time using breaking to dispel the others' magic as fast as they threw it at him.

Play battles didn't overly excite him, not after fighting for his life for real on multiple occasions. They also didn't put him in danger of dying, so you had to take the good with the bad.

Speaking of bad, Maria was still trying to figure out how the ruby ring worked. All she knew for sure was that the gem wasn't a ruby. You'd think after all this time and making so little progress she'd be frustrated, but you'd be wrong. If anything the challenge made her even more excited about the project. It was a damn good thing she took over for him. Otherwise Conryu would have quit by now.

"Listen up." Coach Chort stopped pacing and faced them. "We're leaving for Central this morning for a two-day practice session. You'll be taking on a team of Department wizards put together to mimic the power and abilities of the teams you'll face in the tournament. I have no idea what events they plan to replicate so stay on your toes."

Leslie, the fire wizard, thrust her hand up. "What about our classes tomorrow?"

"You've been excused. Notes on what you missed will be provided when we get back."

Karie, the water wizard, put her hand up. "Is Heather going to be joining us?" She had a serious crush on their stunning assistant coach, not that he blamed her.

"She's supposed to arrive on Monday, assuming she finishes her interviews."

Conryu didn't bother raising his hand. "Who else will be there?"

"Everyone that matters, including a select group of broadcast executives who want to see how good you are and if you'll be a better draw than what we've been putting up the last few years. This practice run is a big deal, so don't screw it up. Fall in behind me." She turned on her heel and marched towards the door.

Conryu glanced at Crystal. "Think she was in the army?"

Crystal flashed a quick smile. "No doubt in my mind."

The group followed their coach down to the train platform. The last of the week's groceries were being unloaded. In front of the supply car was a small passenger cabin. They wouldn't have to sit on bags of onions this trip.

Ten minutes later the train lurched into motion. Trees whizzed by as they raced toward Central. Conryu hadn't been to the capital since last summer when he captured the Society spy. Would anyone try to kill him this visit? Probably not if a bunch of Department wizards were attending to watch their match. He leaned back into his lumpy seat and tried to relax. Security wasn't his responsibility this time.

Coach Chort sat in the front of the car and looked at them. "Remember your training and work together. As long as you do your best you have nothing to be ashamed of."

She stared at Conryu as she said that last bit as if he didn't plan to give it his best. He might not be the most enthusiastic participant, but damned if he was going to hold back and let the team down.

"That book of yours going to be a problem, Koda?" Coach asked.

Conryu looked at Prime. "Are you going to be a problem?"

"No, Master."

"Prime says he won't be a problem."

"I meant wizards with familiars tend to have them targeted by the opposing team. You're only a sophomore, but I assume you know how to share defensive spells?"

"Don't worry about us, Coach. Prime and I have been through some rough situations and come through okay."

She nodded. "Fair enough."

The train arrived at the Department warehouse in just

under half an hour. A gray passenger van with a black penta-gram on the side waited to take them the rest of the way. To where, no one felt the need to explain.

Conryu grimaced when he sat on the hard seat and dropped his bag at his feet. Outside the tinted windows the city grew ever closer. Department headquarters was on their left, but the van bore right. The plot thickened. Maybe they had a super-secure, secret facility arranged for the practice session.

The van pulled up beside the stadium where the Central Yellowjackets baseball team held their games. So much for a secret facility. At least the venue was appropriate for the event.

Beside him Crystal was practically bouncing with excite-ment. "Are you a Yellowjackets fan?" Conryu asked.

"No, where I'm from we bleed Cardinal red. I've just never been to a pro stadium before. I wish we could get some hotdogs and popcorn, but I'll bet the concession stands are shut down."

Conryu glanced around at the huge piles of plowed-up snow. "I'm afraid you might be right. Why don't you swing by after the tournament this summer and we can take in a game at Sentinel Stadium? I don't think Kelsie's ever been either."

"That sounds great."

The group followed Coach Chort through the gates, down a long tunnel that caused their steps to echo, and out onto the field. Even Conryu had to admit as he looked around at the empty seats that being out on the field was kind of cool.

"Reveal."

All around him wards sparkled in his arcane vision. The potent protections should keep any errant spells from damaging the stands. He'd have to be careful not to dispel them.

* * *

Malice Kincade watched this year's team march into the stadium from one of the luxury skyboxes. All the lights were out so no one on the field would notice her. She ignored the plush leather chairs around her, preferring to stand near the window.

Despite her age, Malice had perfect vision thanks to enhancement spells cast over the years by her wizard doctor. In that perfect vision she spotted a familiar figure in black. The arrogant boy that had turned down the honor of donating his genetic material for the betterment of wizardkind. And by that she meant the Kincade family. If Malice believed one thing with all her being, it was that what benefited her family benefited the world. That the world was often too stupid to see that didn't concern her.

Malice's subordinates, along with the network people, huddled together in the box next door. The public relations department was doing their best to hype up the team. Of course, just having Conryu on board did much to pique the reporters' interest. If he put on a good show, everyone should be well pleased. Though whether they were or not didn't concern her any more than the budget cuts did. The Kincade's private research interested her far more than anything the Department had in development.

The lights in the box came on and she hissed. "Turn that off."

"Sorry," a smooth, feminine voice said. "I finished early and decided to see how my team was doing."

"The show is about to begin." Malice glanced at the young, firm figure of Heather James and knew a moment of envy. She snarled it away. The days of her youth had come and gone long

49

ago and she refused to mourn them. "Have you begun your mission?"

"I've laid the groundwork: hints dropped, and initial contact made. I plan to begin phase two after school ends for the year."

"As you think best. Seduction isn't my area of expertise and wasn't even when I was your age. As long as the job gets done, the means don't interest me. How was his initial reaction?"

Heather tossed her hair over her shoulder and her lips curled into a sneer. "It was the same as every man's when they see me for the first time. He recovered faster than most and seemed comfortable after the initial surprise wore off. That was unusual. Most men can barely string two sentences together when they're with me."

"I can imagine."

Out on the field the Department team strode out of the opposite tunnel. The training committee had chosen a pair of relatively simple challenges for the first day of practice. Something the inexperienced team should be able to handle well enough to impress the network executives. That was the theory anyway.

They started with a group casting. The Department team went first and to the surprise of no one Conryu blew their creation away. His strength terrified and intrigued her in equal measure. Was there even an upper limit to his power? There had to be, but she doubted they'd seen it yet. Sooner rather than later she would have to bring him more fully under the Department's control.

His teammates conjured their construct, but it fared no better than their opponents'. The first round ended in a draw.

Heather made a noise that was half sigh and half purr. "He certainly is impressive. You can't tell from here, but he's not bad looking either. I might have taken this job for free if I'd known ahead of time."

"No, you wouldn't. You're a money-hungry slut who wouldn't lift a finger for free, even if it was in your best interest."

Heather laughed. "You know me better than I thought. I'd better go down and cheer on my team. I'm sure having me there watching will spur them on to greater efforts."

"No doubt."

Heather left and she put the conniving whore out of her mind. As long as she got the job done it didn't matter how much she disgusted Malice. And she'd better get it done or she could kiss her precious modeling contract goodbye along with her payment.

* * *

Conryu rolled his shoulders and tried to relax before the next round. There had been a moment when he thought their construct might survive the test, then the dark magic sphere had crashed through and blasted it to bits. They'd still managed a draw so it could have been worse.

An amplified voice came over the loudspeakers. "Round two will be a melee. The battle will end when one team is unable to continue. Lethal force is obviously forbidden. Light magic healers are on hand should there be any accidents. You have five minutes to plan your strategy."

Coach motioned them over and they huddled around her.

"Wait for me!" Heather came running out of the tunnel in her aqua robe. "I finished early and hurried to join you."

She smiled in Conryu's direction and ignored Coach Chort's look of annoyance.

"Okay, now that we're all here," Coach said. "We need a plan. I hadn't expected them to call for a melee so I didn't think much about it. Not that it would have mattered. Basically, you need to react to what your opponents do. The team that adapts the quickest wins. The best advice I can give you is to back each other up and don't be afraid to use your strongest spells. Koda, it's your job to create openings for the others so the pressure's on. Don't screw up. Good luck."

The huddle broke and he stared at Coach Chort. What a lousy pep talk. He turned to find Heather a few feet away. She pecked him on the cheek.

"What was that for?"

"Luck. It's your first match, don't be nervous."

"Thanks."

She joined the coach on the sidelines. The voice on the loud speaker counted down from ten. The others cast defensive spells and Conryu joined in, covering himself and Prime with Cloak of Darkness. That would stop any but the most powerful spells.

He glanced at the others as magic crackled around them. He was the youngest one here yet he knew the easiest way for them to win was for him to cast Reaper's Cloak and wade into the enemy. A few solid blows would end the match in a hurry.

"Two."

"Are we allowed to fly?" Emily, the wind wizard, asked.

"One."

"No one said we weren't," Leslie said, a fire aura crackling around her.

"Fight!"

Conryu raised his hand. "Break!"

While they were debating the enemy fire wizard had launched a fireball at the gathered team.

"Spread out so they can't hit us all with a single spell." Conryu suited his action to his word and darted right.

A lightning bolt crackled past him and fizzled on the wards. "Earth magic, Master."

Conryu leapt over a pair of hands that erupted out of the ground. The girls were running around like chickens with their heads cut off, dodging spells, and making the occasional weak counter.

The Department team looked totally at ease, their dark wizard negating anything that got close. Maybe he should give them something to think about.

"The chill wind of Hades blow and slay. Death rides in the blackened air, Reaper's Gale!" Conryu waved his hand at the enemy wizards and a wind kicked up. Black, barely visible threads rode the breeze. One strand grazed the ground and turned the snow to brackish water.

The Department's dark magic wizard hurled a Dispel sphere at the approaching gale, but it only erased a small portion.

"Run!" the enemy team's earth wizard shouted.

They scattered and ceased the barrage of spells that had been pelting his team. Conryu left his spell to run its course and ran over to the others. "That bought us a minute, but we need to hit them before they recover."

"What did you have in mind?" Crystal asked.

"How about we send a pair of stone behemoths after them? That should create enough chaos to let the others pick them off."

Crystal looked around. "Who's going to cast the second spell?"

"I will. I know Stone Behemoth, though I've only cast it twice."

The others were muttering amongst themselves. On the far side of the field another section of his spell collapsed.

"We're running out of time," Conryu said. "If we're going to do this, we need to do it now."

"I say we try it," Karie said.

The moment one person agreed the others fell in behind her. Conryu looked at Crystal and nodded.

She chanted first.

While her behemoth was forming Conryu cast, "Understanding is the true path to peace, Perfect Translation."

Once he could speak to his construct, he cast a second time. "Oh Mother Earth, give birth to a child of stone to serve this unworthy wizard, Stone Behemoth."

The ground trembled and soon a twenty-foot-tall giant stood in front of him. He pointed at the regrouping wizards across the way. "Crush them!"

His behemoth stomped towards them, shaking the field with each stride. Crystal's smaller creature fell in beside it and everyone else got behind them.

"Prime, give me a bird's-eye view."

"Yes, Master." Prime flew up and peeked over the construct's shoulder just in time to see a lightning blast streak in and slam into Conryu's behemoth.

The earth was so dense it barely flinched. Using Prime's sight as his own Conryu watched the distance close between them and the Department team.

He tapped Karie on the shoulder. "Their wind wizard is on the far right. When I signal, jump out and blast her."

The fire wizard nodded and began murmuring a spell. It wasn't one Conryu knew, but he hoped it would get the job done.

Three more steps then... "Now!"

Karie leapt out and hurled a stream of flames. The blast slammed into a wind barrier and knocked the wizard into the stadium wall with enough force to knock her out.

One down, five to go.

The enemy water wizard spotted Karie in the open and vulnerable and began to cast.

Conryu darted out, grabbed Karie by the collar, and yanked her back just ahead of a barrage of ice blades.

Karie swallowed hard. "Thanks."

He nodded and returned his focus to Prime. The behemoths were only a few strides from the enemy wizards. Their dark wizard was chanting and building power. If her Dispel hit, they'd lose their cover.

Conryu grinned. "Crystal! Have your behemoth fall forward."

She stared at him for a moment then her eyes widened and she nodded.

At Conryu's mental command his construct did a belly flop toward the Department wizards followed a moment later by Crystal's.

As they fell, he ended the spell that held the construct together. The dense humanoid form collapsed. It looked like a dump truck had backed up to the wizards and emptied its load on them. A couple heads popped out here and there, but everyone else was totally covered.

"The Academy team wins," the voice on the loudspeaker said. "Now dig them out of there before they suffocate."

Looked like they'd won their first match. Conryu and Crystal shared a high five and chanted in the language of earth. The Department wizards probably wouldn't like getting rescued by their opponents, but at least they'd be able to breathe.

* * *

So much for a night in the big city. The van bounced its way back to the train depot. The sun hadn't even set yet and the team was returning to the Academy. On one hand, it was kind of a drag, but on the other they'd won their match.

After they finished freeing the last Department wizard it became clear that they were in no shape to have another match the next day. Every one of them had broken bones, and their unfortunate light wizard got dirt in her lungs so she could barely breathe.

In the front of the van Coach Chort stared out the window, watching the city go by. The tendons on the side of her neck stood out as did a bunched muscle in her jaw. She looked pissed about something and he suspected it was him.

Conryu took a breath and steeled himself for a thorough chewing out. "Sorry about the match, Coach. I didn't realize how much dirt was in the behemoth I created."

"Don't worry about it. This sort of thing happens in the tournament all the time. What's got me angry is that the suit I talked to while you were cleaning up only said we did okay. Okay! Did he not see the biggest Stone Behemoth ever? In my thirty years as a wizard I've never seen one that big. Do you know what the son of a bitch said when I pointed that out?"

Conryu shook his head.

"He said it would have been nice if it was created by my earth wizard instead of my dark wizard. I said you were on the same team and as long as we won, what difference did it make? He shook his head and said wizards should stick to their specialty. Can you believe that? This putz that doesn't know wind magic from flatulence is telling me what wizards should be doing on my team. I nearly decked him."

"What stopped you?" Crystal asked.

"He's the one that hired me and I figured if I punched him I wouldn't get paid. A wizard's got to eat after all."

That brought a chuckle from the team and some of the tension drained away. Maybe Coach Chort wasn't so bad. Intense, certainly, but not bad.

The van pulled up beside the train and they transferred over. The half-hour trip passed in near silence as everyone digested what had just happened. They'd had their first match ever and won.

He'd feared they might think he overstepped his bounds when he took control of the battle, but no one seemed to, not even Caroline, the light magic wizard that was supposed to be this year's team captain. In fact, they almost seemed relieved someone had taken charge. They didn't have a single person returning from last year's team and, frankly, even if they did he wasn't sure a proven failure would have been welcome as leader.

The train approached the Academy and Conryu got an idea. No one expected them until tomorrow. This would be a perfect time to surprise Maria. They hadn't been alone in forever.

They piled out of the train and Coach told them they'd resume regular training next Sunday. Conryu waved to the others and hurried toward the dorm. He strode through the cafeteria and over to the kitchens.

Twenty pots bubbled on the stove, stirred by invisible spirits. Three women in red robes oversaw everything. The oldest-looking of the group marched toward him waving her hands like she was shooing a cat.

"Dinner will be ready in half an hour. You're welcome to wait in the cafeteria."

"I was hoping to get two plates early so I could surprise my girlfriend with a romantic dinner." He flashed his best smile. "Couldn't you help me out?"

"It's against school rules."

"I won't tell anyone, I swear. Please? Maria and I haven't had a quiet dinner together in ages."

Her stern expression cracked and he knew he had her. "Don't think this is going to be a regular thing. Hold on."

She moved back into the kitchen and spoke to the others who broke into a fit of giggling. Between them they soon had two plates filled and covered with cloths. A pitcher of water and two glasses joined the food on the tray and she brought the whole thing over to him.

"Have fun."

Conryu grinned. "Thanks. You're the best."

He made off with his prize and hurried to his room. The moment he arrived he set the tray down and jotted a quick note. "Are you there, little one?"

The pixie swirled around him and materialized on his shoulder. She hugged his neck and he smiled.

"Can you take this to Maria? You know her, she's come to see me before."

The pixie nodded, took his message, and flew away. Hopefully she didn't just ignore it.

Now to get ready. He used earth magic to enhance his strength and moved the table in front of the bed. Next the chair went on the opposite side. A burst of will summoned two flickering flames that floated above the table. Not exactly candlelight, but it would do. He flipped the lights out and nodded. Not bad.

Since the library wasn't that far from his room it didn't take long for a knock to sound on his door. Conryu leapt to his feet and opened it.

Maria stood outside, arms crossed. "What is it? I was in the middle of reading a treatise on fire realm royalty."

He opened the door wide and stepped aside. "Surprise."

She stared for a moment. "What's all this?"

"Dinner. How long has it been since we had an hour all to ourselves? We got back early, so I thought I'd surprise you. Come on, before it gets cold."

She entered and he closed the door behind her. Conryu pulled the chair out for her then sat opposite on the bed. "It's not the best, but—"

"It's perfect." She lifted the lid on her plate and he poured them each a glass of water.

His chicken had cooled a little and he assumed hers had as well. Conryu focused and called on a wisp of fire magic. In a blink the food was piping hot again.

They ate in silence for a minute, just enjoying being alone together. Finally Maria asked, "How did your practice match go?"

"We won. We also almost killed the Department team, but no one seemed overly upset. Unfortunately, they weren't in any shape to go another round. What about you, having any luck?"

"Some. I figured out what the stone is. You'll never guess."

He loved seeing her so excited. "Don't keep me in suspense."

"It's blood. The crystalized blood of an efreet prince. I also know what the ring does. First, anyone that wears it gets a boost to their fire magic power. Second, and I haven't actually figured out how to do this yet, you should be able to use the blood as a link to the efreet it belongs to so you can summon and control him. I need to figure out which spirit it is and his true name. Once I learn that I can summon him."

"Are you sure?" Conryu hated to rain on her parade, but he feared Maria's excitement might be overwhelming her good sense. "Maybe it would be better to have a fire wizard do it."

She smiled in the firelight. "That's the beauty of the device. It contains all the magic necessary to summon and compel the spirit as long as you understand how to use it properly. Even the weakest wizard could wield it."

"That's amazing."

"I know, right? Elf artifacts are amazing. I think I may have found my calling."

"What calling?"

"Relic Hunter." She was practically bouncing in her seat. "I've had more fun this past month doing research than I have with anything else we've tried. I can easily imagine spending the rest of my life working with these items."

He'd never seen her so eager, especially about something as dangerous as relic hunting. For every ten teams that went out to explore an elf ruin, only one returned with an artifact and only three returned alive. He would always support Maria, but this struck him as one case where perhaps he should try to discourage her. He loved her too much to want her taking such crazy risks. That was his job.

* * *

"Are you sure that's a good idea? Relic hunting doesn't have a very high survival rate."

Conryu's obvious dismay at her announcement made Maria smile. "You don't know much about the Relic Hunters organization do you?"

"I know the survival rate of the teams going out into the ruins and it sucks." He tossed his napkin on the table. "I wouldn't be able to sleep if you were out in the field with one of those teams."

"Well, you're in luck." She got up, came around the table, and lay down on the bed facing him. "I have no interest in field work. I'm interested in research."

From his blank expression he clearly had no idea what she was talking about. Maria patted the mattress beside her and he lay down, draping one arm around her. She groaned. God that felt good. It had been far too long since they enjoyed some quiet time together.

"Do you want to fill me in?" he said.

"The Relic Hunters organization is a huge, multinational group with headquarters in Central, London, Sydney, and Neo Tokyo. Not only do they send out the teams that give them their name, but they also catalogue, research, and store relics as well as non-magical items. Over half their staff is made up of normal people studying elf culture. There are archeologists, biologists, chemists, you name it. Information is shared with the governments of the four nations and they provide funding."

"That doesn't sound so bad." He relaxed and Maria snuggled into him. "So you'd work in Central?"

"Probably. Don't worry. We've still got two and a half years of school. I might change my mind again."

"If I found a bike shop in Central, I could work near you. We could find an apartment, live like a normal couple."

It would be nice, but she didn't believe for a moment there was any chance of it happening. It was sweet that he still clung to his dream, but even Conryu couldn't be so stubborn that he imagined a future for himself that didn't involve magic.

Maria rolled over so she was facing him. "I'm afraid you're setting yourself up for disappointment. You're too valuable to the Department for them to simply let you walk away after graduation."

"I know." The words came out as a reluctant groan. "But can't I pretend, just for a little while?"

"Sure." She kissed him. "You can pretend as long as you want, but I'm not certain how long the world will allow you your illusions."

Conryu's smile held an edge. "Sometimes you can compel the world to see things your way, if you have strength enough."

She held him tighter. Thinking like that might get him in real trouble. If Conryu decided to go against the Department, she really didn't know what might happen. All she knew was a lot of people might get hurt.

* * *

Lady Tiger adjusted her crimson gown as she rode up the elevator to the top floor of the London Museum of Magic. She checked her reflection in the polished brass of the door. Without her mask she felt naked, but she couldn't exactly meet with an Art Society matron dressed as a Hierarch. The pompous old bat didn't even realize she was a wizard. All she knew was that Lady Tish, as she called herself, had made a million-pound donation to help cover the cost of the Magic Gala.

And that was all she wanted or needed to know in order to grant this meeting. Previewing the space, she called it. Showing off the view of the city more likely.

Lady Tiger adjusted the gold ring on her right hand. The ring held a light magic enchantment that would prevent any

Ministry wizards from reading her thoughts. Not that she expected to meet any at this little get-together. Still, better safe than sorry. If she had to fight her way out of the museum, it would make her task much harder down the road.

The bell chimed and the doors slid aside revealing a large open room with windows on all four sides. From here she could see the entire city sprawling in every direction. Her lip quirked as she imagined the forty Blessed Army soldiers she'd already delivered making their way through the slums, meeting up with their anarchist allies, and distributing the weapons they'd brought with them. It would be quite a show and she badly wanted to get it underway.

"Dear Lady Tish." She'd been so wrapped up in her thoughts she hadn't even noticed the portly matron standing at a bank of windows.

Mrs. Pollock wore all purple as was her habit. The first time they'd met at a cocktail party two years ago she'd claimed with a wink that it was the color of royalty. To Lady Tiger she looked like a giant plum waddling toward her. She suppressed a shudder, plastered on her best smile, and held out her hands.

The old woman took them in her white-gloved hands and gave a light squeeze. "I'm so glad you made it. As our most generous donor I felt it incumbent upon me to give you an up-close look at the space we'll be using. Isn't the view spectacular?"

"Indeed. I was so impressed I didn't even notice you at first. A bit empty though, don't you think?"

Mrs. Pollock sighed. "Yes. There's so much still to do. But in three months this floor will be transformed into a replica of an elf ruin. We've even hired a retired Relic Hunter to advise us. We'll be the toast of London, rest assured."

"I'd feel better if I could see some of the display pieces."

Lady Tiger knew what her host would say before she said it, but no harm in trying.

"I wish that was possible, but the Ministry is ever so fussy about security. It's as if they imagine we'll snatch them and run off. Foolish, but what can you do? The items we're planning to show aren't even on the premises yet and won't be until the night of our opening. They'll remain under guard the whole time and return to secure storage at the end of the evening."

"I'm pleased they're taking every precaution." Inside, Lady Tiger seethed. If the Ministry kept a sizable force of guards on site, it would make it far more difficult for her to get the fragment. She'd figure out a way to do it. Under no circumstances would she allow Lady Wolf to show her up.

5

YEAR END

Conryu yawned and stared at the ceiling. The team had its last practice yesterday and he was still beat. Lucky for him finals were coming up in a few days so the teachers had given everyone some time to study on their own. All he had to do this year was summon a spirit of each element and show his ability to control it.

That was beyond simple for him since they all acted like he shared their alignment. Even that golden lion thing he'd summoned last week with St. Seraphim had purred like a kitten and lowered its head for a good scratch behind the ears. He couldn't imagine any way anyone might sabotage his test this year. Hopefully that didn't indicate a lack of imagination on his part.

Someone knocked on his door and Conryu hopped off the bed. He wasn't expecting anyone today. Maria was buried up to her ears in books. She still hadn't figured out which efreet prince was bound to the ring, but it wasn't for a lack of trying. He'd suggested two weeks ago that she move on to one of the other artifacts, but as expected she refused to give up until she worked it out.

He opened the door and found Kelsie outside, staring at her shoes and twisting her robe in her fingers.

"What's up?"

She dropped the section of robe she'd been holding and looked up at him. "I'm going to fail the final, I just know it."

"Since your family isn't speaking to you, I assume it wasn't a call from your mother that messed you up. Come on in and tell me about it."

She scooted past him and settled on the edge of the bed. "It's fire spirits. I'm afraid they're going to burn me and my fear's screwing up my binding spells. Mrs. Smith says I need to be more confident if I want to control the spirits properly, but I can't manage it."

"We don't have much time to get this straightened out. What kind of spirit did you summon?"

"A fire kitten. It's the cutest thing, but hot."

Conryu scratched his chin and dropped into his chair. All fire spirits were hot, so if she wanted one that wasn't she was out of luck.

"What if I summon one and you can play with it? That way you'll see it won't burn you by accident."

"I guess we could try that. Are you summoning a fire kitten too?"

"No, I'm summoning a phoenix yearling. What's the name of your spirit?"

He cast the translation spell and she told him its name. The spell didn't like it, but it came out to roughly Fire Paws.

They cleared a space in the middle of his room and he drew an appropriate circle. It wasn't really necessary for him, but better to cast the spell by the book for Kelsie's sake. When the circle was in place, he focused on the kitten's name then cast, "From the hottest realm I call you, child of fire. Appear and serve a loyal ally of flame. Fire Summoning!"

A flame burst to life in the center of the circle and transformed into the most adorable little red-and-orange kitten he'd ever seen. Little wisps of flame rose off the tips of its ears as it paced around the circle.

"Are you seriously afraid of that?" Conryu asked.

"It's crazy, I understand, but he's made of fire. It's like sticking my hand into an oven."

Conryu finished the binding and dismissed the circle. The fire kitten ran up and rubbed its cheek against his shin. He crouched and stroked its back. The spirit felt warm, but not hot and more solid than he'd expected for a being made of fire.

The kitten reared up on its hind legs and waved its paws at him. Conryu grinned and scooped it up. He was going to have to summon one of these little guys to keep him warm next winter. He murmured to it and his spell translated the words into the language of fire.

Kelsie watched the proceedings with a nervous smile. He held the kitten out to her and her eyes widened.

"Go on, he's not burning me, is he?"

"No, but spirits like you. Who knows what might happen when you let go."

"I told him to behave. What's wrong, don't you trust my binding?" If he made it a matter of trusting him instead of the spirit, maybe she'd get over her fear.

"Of course I trust you." She raised her hands partway, paused, steeled herself, then raised them the rest of the way.

"Good." Conryu set the kitten in her arms and it snuggled in.

She looked up at him with wide eyes. "He's almost as cuddly as a real kitten. So soft and warm."

"Right? Are you still scared?"

"No. I feel silly for having been worried at all."

"Cool." Conryu released the spell and the fire kitten vanished. "Why don't we try having you summon one of your own? If you can do it here, you can do it at the final."

She chewed her lip and wouldn't look at him. He recognized that expression.

"What's wrong?"

"I'm not sure if I'm supposed to tell you."

"Did someone order you not to?"

"No."

"Then tell me."

She took a breath then nodded. "I talked to Dean Blane yesterday. Grandmother is coming to observe the finals."

Conryu groaned. So much for his hope that no one could mess up his test this year. "What does she want?"

Kelsie shrugged. "As far as Dean Blane knows, just to see where the students stand. At least that's what she said, but I'm not sure the dean believes it."

Conryu wasn't sure either, but it was out of his hands. They couldn't exactly bar the Head of the Department of Magic from the campus. He was doubly glad he hadn't let Maria hang on to the elf artifact.

"How about you try that summoning now?"

"Okay. I'll show Grandmother how much I've learned. Maybe she'll finally treat me with something other than disdain."

Conryu wasn't sure Malice knew how to treat people with anything but disdain. Still, he didn't want to discourage her. "That's the spirit. Now summon that kitten back."

* * *

M alice hadn't been to the Academy campus in three years. The train slowed as it approached the platform. She'd insisted they hook up a luxury car even though the ride only took half an hour. She did it more to remind them who they answered to than because she cared about gold-plated fixtures and calf-leather seats. It was important to remind your subordinates who controlled their fate; it kept them properly grateful when she didn't turn her gaze their way.

Speaking of people who needed to remember their place, Dean Blane stood on the platform waiting to greet her. The woman looked ridiculous in the form of a little girl. Malice still didn't know why she bothered transforming herself like that. The appearance of a child was no more appealing than that of an old woman.

No matter, the idiosyncrasies of the school's head didn't concern her. The place continued to churn out competent, and more importantly loyal, wizards and as long as it did that she didn't care if the dean transformed herself into a howler monkey.

Malice glanced at her two aides, distant Kincade cousins for whom she'd arranged jobs at the Department. They were both reasonably strong and absolutely obedient. Either of them would step in front of a death spell for her and Malice expected nothing less.

She levered herself out of the soft seat and grimaced when her hip caught. Damned useless body. Even light magic healing didn't last these days. It wouldn't be long before she'd need to decide between undeath and the real thing. But not today.

"Welcome to the Academy, Director Kincade," Dean Blane

said when she stepped out onto the platform. "I trust your ride was smooth."

"The train is always smooth. When do the sophomores have their final?"

"In just under an hour. I've arranged private seating for you as requested. I think you'll be pleased with how far Kelsie has come."

Malice snorted. "Who cares about that ungrateful child? Conryu interests me and no one else. I assume you heard about what he did to the Department team that went up against him and the Academy team."

"Yes, I'm glad everyone made a full recovery. I'm sure he didn't mean to hurt anyone. That boy has a gentle soul."

Malice waved a bony hand. "I don't care about that either. He summoned a Stone Behemoth that stood over twenty feet tall and according to Coach Chort he wasn't even using his full strength. Twenty feet! I don't know more than a handful of earth-aligned wizards that could do that, much less a dark-aligned one. He needs closer supervision than we've been providing."

"Um, the thing is, Conryu is aligned to all elements. Just because he's strongest in dark doesn't mean he isn't also strong in everything else. Lumping him in with normal dark wizards is a mistake."

Malice glared at the tiny woman. If there was one thing she didn't like, it was being corrected. To her credit Dean Blane didn't flinch from the look. Malice had turned the knees of heads of state to jelly with that stare.

"I'm aware of his unique situation." She waved Dean Blane off. "Let's get inside. I'd like to keep this visit quiet and standing out here where everyone can see me isn't going to help with that."

Dean Blane led the way across the campus to the main building. Malice hobbled along behind, grimacing with her determination to show no weakness. She barely noticed the passages they followed, the only thing that caught her attention was the chair waiting in a small room overlooking the auditorium.

Malice barely held in a sigh of relief as she took the weight off her feet.

"If I'd have known you were bringing guests with you I'd have arranged for extra chairs. If you give me a moment I can have more here in short order," Dean Blane said.

Malice waved a dismissive hand. "They'll be fine. I don't intend to stay here a moment longer than necessary."

"We usually have Conryu go last, but if you'd like I can send him out first."

"No. Do nothing that might reveal my presence. The boy and I don't get on well and I'd just as soon avoid dealing with him today."

Dean Blane bowed. "As you wish. Please make yourself comfortable. It will be about an hour and a half."

With that final pronouncement, the chattering nuisance left her in peace. Five minutes later the first girl stepped out on stage and performed her summoning spells. The spirits were weak things, but typical for a wizard just starting her training.

The process continued in monotonous fashion for far too long. Kelsie came and went, passing her final with ease. That surprised Malice and in a distant corner of her heart, a part she seldom acknowledged existed, pleased her as well.

Perhaps they'd underestimated the girl. After almost a full year with no access to the Kincade fortune, Malice would have bet a substantial amount that Kelsie would have come back begging to enter their good graces once more. It hadn't happened that way and her daughter wasn't at all happy. She'd either need to invite Kelsie back, which would be a sign of weakness, or name a new heir from the rather poor selection of prospects.

Family politics would have to wait for another day. Conryu had just stepped out on stage. This was what she'd come to see. What sort of spirits would he summon? She doubted he'd be content with minor spirits.

He started with light magic and proved her right, summoning a Golden Lion that towered a foot over his head. The giant beast growled and for a moment she thought he might get devoured on stage. Instead it lowered its head and he scratched between its ears. What she'd taken for growling got louder and she realized it was purring.

A Golden Lion, a divine spirit that served as a guardian of the gates of Heaven, was purring like a kitten and submitting with seeming great pleasure to being petted by a dark-aligned wizard.

No, not simply dark aligned. She needed to view him through the lens Dean Blane provided. Assuming he was aligned with all elements the lion's reaction made perfect sense.

When the next two spirits reacted the same as the first she finally understood exactly how his unique alignment functioned. Each spirit treated him like he shared their alignment and no one else's. It was like they couldn't sense his connection to the other elements.

While Malice couldn't understand how that was possible, no other explanation made sense. Her new knowledge made the trip out here well worth it. Now Malice just had to figure out how to make the information serve her.

And she would figure it out. Her lips curved into a cruel

smile. All things served her, one way or another.

* * *

Conryu yawned and stretched as he walked toward the just-arrived train. Everyone's bags were floating along behind him. He'd insisted Dean Blane teach him that spell and he absolutely loved it. Overhead the summer sun shone bright and warm, and a little breeze ruffled the girls' hair. You couldn't have asked for a nicer day to end the year.

Finals had gone off without a hitch and only three girls in the whole school failed. Dean Blane said that was a record. Conryu's test took only fifteen minutes and no fire-breathing monsters tried to kill him. As Maria liked to say, that was the way finals were supposed to go.

Given all that, he should've been thrilled. Instead, it felt like the real test was about to begin. He was attending a news conference in three days and two days after that boarding a flight to the Kingdom of the Isles for the tournament. He would have preferred to travel by portal, but they had ordinary people traveling with them and the Department wanted everyone to stay together. He'd never flown in a plane before, so that might actually be interesting.

"Penny for your thoughts," Maria said.

He'd gotten so caught up in his musings that he'd forgotten she was there for a moment. "Just thinking about things. Looks like I'm in for another interesting summer."

"Hopefully not as interesting as last year."

"You can say that again. The tournament's tough, but no one has died in over a century. I like those odds."

"Me too." Maria slipped her hand into his and gave a squeeze. "Do you guys have a chance of winning?"

"I'd say so. Coach thinks we do. At our last practice she said we did acceptable. That's high praise."

They reached the train and followed Kelsie and Anya to the cabin they'd been assigned. Given the lack of attacks and his ability to defend himself, Conryu no longer got a special room surrounded by protective wards. His movement also wasn't restricted during travel anymore, not that he had any great desire to wander the aisles.

The little group had barely gotten comfortable when the train lurched into motion. Across from him Kelsie was grinning from ear to ear.

"What's got you so happy?" he asked.

"Just thinking how nice it was to pass this year's final on my own merit instead of having to rely on you." Her eyes widened. "Not that I didn't appreciate the help with the fire kitten."

"Don't worry, I'm glad to help any time you need it." He turned to Anya. "Do you and your mom have any plans for the summer?"

"No, we're just going to play it by ear. It'll be good to spend a few weeks together instead of just a night at a time."

"Sounds nice." Conryu would have rather hung out with vampires than reporters.

They spent the rest of the trip talking about nothing in particular. It was relaxing, hanging out with his friends, no threats, no hidden agendas, just pleasant conversation.

It couldn't last, however. Ten minutes from the Sentinel City station Prime said, "Quite a large crowd."

Conryu got up and joined the scholomantic at the window. Even from this distance dozens of antennas were visible. It looked like all the press in the city had turned out to greet him. There was supposed to be a press conference in two days, what did the hyenas want here?

"I wonder if hell hounds would be good at herding reporters," Conryu said, more to himself than to the others.

"Hell hounds are better at tearing things apart," Prime said.

"Don't tempt me. This is going to suck."

Maria moved to stand beside him. "That's more than when we left the first time."

"Looks like it. Do you suppose if I say 'no comment' enough times they'll take the hint?"

"No, do you?"

He blew out a sigh. "No, I don't either. Mrs. Umbra suggested I fry all their cameras and microphones, but I'm afraid that might not be the best idea. Satisfying, but not the best idea."

The train slowed, so they returned to their seats. Half a minute later it stopped and students began piling out onto the platform. Conryu renewed his spell and the luggage fell in behind him.

He'd barely taken two steps out of the train when flash bulbs started going off and unintelligible questions came hurtling his way. At the edge of the platform a group of about thirty reporters and their associated cameramen jostled for position. It looked like a Black Friday line outside the mall.

"How the hell are we going to get through that gang?" he asked no one in particular.

Conryu was still debating which spells might work best to create a path when a familiar voice shouted his name.

He shifted his gaze further up the platform and there stood Heather James dressed pretty as you please in jeans and a white blouse. He must have been really distracted not to notice her.

"What's she doing here?" Maria gave voice to his question.

"Beats me. No one said to expect her." He shrugged, and,

ignoring the barrage of questions, walked down to meet Heather at the farthest turnstile. "What's up?"

She flashed her perfect smile. "I have it on good authority you have a rough relationship with the press. I'm here to smooth things over. Just follow my lead and don't say anything. The rest of you stay a little ways behind us. Once the reporters are focused on Conryu and I, you should be able to sneak past."

Maria's scowl said she wanted to argue, but Heather's plan was a good one, for Maria and the others at any rate.

"It'll be okay." Conryu whispered in the language of wind, transferring the spell levitating the luggage to Maria. "Wish me luck."

Before Maria had a chance to speak, Heather grabbed his arm and dragged him toward the waiting nest of vipers. Whether accidental or intentional, she pressed her ample chest against his upper arm.

He forced himself not to react, instead focusing on the lights pointed his way and the faces shouting at him. They all bellowed at once so that he couldn't make out any of their questions even if he wanted to answer them.

"Come on, everyone," Heather said. "You know better than to try to get a scoop before the press conference. I'll overlook it this time, but anyone that tries again will have their credentials pulled and then you'll get nothing."

There was considerable grumbling, but she stared down anyone that looked her way. It was quite impressive. She must have had a lot of practice.

"Now make a path so our star player can get home and prepare for the big match. You wouldn't want him arriving in London without getting enough rest, would you?"

"I thought keeping him from resting was your job!" a male reporter at the rear of the pack shouted.

She grinned and squeezed his arm tighter. More cameras flashed. Conryu caught her eye and raised an eyebrow. Heather just winked. What sort of game was she playing?

Finally, the press let them through. A lot of the returning students and their families had already cleared out making it way easier for him to spot his mom, Mr. Kane, and the girls.

As soon as they got free of the press, Conryu disengaged himself from Heather's grasp. "Thanks for getting me through that. My mom's over there. See you later."

"At the press conference day after tomorrow. I'll be joining you to handle any tricky questions."

"And here I thought your job was to make sure I showed up at all."

"That too." Heather broke off and headed toward the parking lot, throwing a wave over her shoulder.

So much for his hope that this summer would be less complicated. Somehow dealing with shadow beasts sounded easier than handling Heather.

As soon as he reached them Mom rushed over and hugged him. "I missed you, sweetheart."

He shook hands with Mr. Kane and Maria examined his arm.

"What's wrong?"

"I'm looking for sucker marks. That octopus was all over you."

"She was a little clingy." He shrugged, not wanting to make a big deal about it. "Shall we get out of here?"

Once they'd loaded the car they took off. Mr. Kane looked at him in the rearview mirror. "I forgot to mention this earlier, but you can take three people with you to London for free as guests. I wanted to let you know so you can decide who you want to bring."

He glanced at Maria. "What do you say?"

She didn't have time to answer before Mr. Kane said, "No need to use one of your spots for Maria. We're all going as part of the official Department delegation."

"That takes care of that," Conryu said. "Kelsie?"

"I'm in."

"Mom, any chance you and Dad will come?"

"Sorry, sweetheart. I'm swamped at work and you know your father. We'll watch your matches on tv, I promise."

He looked to Anya, but she shook her head. Conryu didn't figure she'd want to give up a week with her mother, but wanted to ask anyway. "I'm sure Jonny will want to go. That leaves me one short."

"I'm sure you'll find someone," Maria said. "It shouldn't be hard to give away an all-expenses-paid trip to London."

* * *

At ten o'clock Conryu pulled into the Department parking lot and guided his bike into the first spot he found. The press vans were there already. A quick glance around the lot revealed Mr. Kane's car, but no other ones that he recognized. The moment the engine stopped Prime flew out of his saddlebag and glared at him. At least some things in this crazy world stayed the same.

Conryu took a breath and tried to focus. He'd woken up before dawn that morning, too anxious to sleep. He couldn't see any way for this to end well. Perhaps if he kept his mouth shut and let Heather answer all the questions.

On the plus side, when he'd grabbed his phone off the night-stand and flicked it on he found one new message, from Crystal. She'd gotten in touch with Sonja and the little fire wizard was keen to join the trip. Unfortunately, both Crystal's parents and her little brother wanted to go too so she didn't have a free spot. Conryu had grinned and tapped out a response. Maybe it was fate that he hadn't found a third person to bring along yet.

He grabbed his key out of the ignition and started for the doors. The best part of his extended spell repertoire was that he didn't need to wear a helmet anymore; Diamond Skin offered better protection. Of course, he could have just flown, but he wasn't ready to abandon his bike yet.

"Ready to face the vultures, pal?"

"If any of them become too much of a nuisance, Master, I'll bite their faces off."

Conryu grinned at the image. "I can see the headlines now: 'Demon Book Attempts to Devour Local Reporter.' Seriously though, don't do that."

He pulled the door open and grimaced. The entire lobby resembled the room where the president and his advisors met with the press. At one end was a raised table covered in gray cloth. Four chairs with microphones in front of them ran the length of it. Who was the fourth one for?

It appeared that every reporter from the train station had shown up here. Apparently Heather hadn't pulled anyone's credentials. Pity.

Now, where was everybody? Heather and Mr. Kane were supposed to be leading this wretched affair.

"Conryu, my boy!"

"Oh, no." He turned slowly toward the doors like some poor victim in a horror movie. Striding in wearing his tweed jacket, white hair going every which way, was Angus. Why in heaven's name was the professor here?

Angus clapped him on the back. "I can't tell you how excited I was when I learned you'd be competing in the tournament."

"I'll bet. Why are you here again?"

"I'll be traveling to London with you. The Department hired me as a color commentator for the broadcast. I am the foremost expert on male wizards after all."

"Right." This deal just kept getting worse and worse.

"Master, by the elevators."

As soon as Prime spoke Conryu spotted Heather waving at him. She had on her aqua wizard's robe. He marched over to join her, Angus a step behind.

"Where have you been?" Heather asked. "Never mind, you need to get changed."

"Why?"

"Because you don't look like a wizard, you look like a delinquent."

He looked down at his jeans and black t-shirt. "This is what I always wear. I'm here to talk, not give a magic show."

"Just humor me. All you need to do is throw a black robe over your street clothes, just like at the Academy. Okay?"

"Fine."

She dragged him down to a storage closet leaving Angus behind. Heather pulled out a blessedly plain black robe which he tossed over his head. "Happy?"

The elevator chimed and Mr. Kane stepped out. He had on a crisp suit in Department gray. "Oh, good, you're both ready. Don't worry, Conryu, I've only scheduled half an hour for questions so we'll have you out of here in no time."

"Thanks. Do I need to fill out a form or something for my three guests?"

"No, just have them arrive with you and everything will be fine. Shall we?"

Mr. Kane didn't wait for a reply, instead marching straight toward the table. Heather fell in beside Conryu, so close that their shoulders practically rubbed.

They reached the table and Conryu ended up between Heather and Angus, beauty and the beast as the saying went.

Mr. Kane raised his hands and the reporters fell silent. "Ladies and gentlemen, thank you for coming. I'm sure you have a lot of questions so I'll keep this short. I'm pleased to be joined on stage by the youngest Alliance team member in fifty years, Conryu Koda. Also with us today is Assistant Coach Heather James. I'm sure all of you are familiar with both of them as they've made quite a name for themselves. With Conryu on the team and Heather helping with the coaching I think we have an excellent chance to reverse our fortunes this year. The floor is now open for questions."

Thirty hands shot up. Mr. Kane pointed at a red-faced man in a yellow-brown suit. "Sean, go ahead."

"Thanks, Chief Kane. Conryu, how are you feeling about being a member of such a prestigious team? Given your youth and inexperience it must be daunting."

Since no one was going to be trying to kill him, Conryu wasn't nervous in the least. "I'm just going to do my best and hope I can help."

"So you're not nervous?" Sean asked.

"No."

Conryu and the reporter stared at each other until it became clear neither of them had anything more to say. What did the guy want? Conryu had fought demons, undead, shadow beasts, and dragon monsters of various sorts; play fighting with a bunch of other students didn't get his pulse racing.

"Next?" Mr. Kane asked when the silence had stretched to an uncomfortable point. "Samantha, go ahead."

A cute brunette with short hair and glasses stood up.

"Heather." Conryu slumped with relief. "You've spent the bulk of your time traveling the Alliance doing interviews. Given your lack of success as team captain, wouldn't it be more realistic to say you were acting as press liaison rather than assistant coach?"

If the dig bothered her Heather hid it well. She turned her thousand-watt smile on the reporter and said, "I'm here to help Coach Chort and the team in any way I can. If doing interviews to drum up interest is the most useful thing I can do, I'm happy to do it. Though I like to think I have more to offer given my experience at the tournament."

Before Mr. Kane could call on another reporter a woman at the rear of the group leapt to her feet. "Amanda Jenkins, Sentinel Enquirer. Is there any truth to the rumors that the two of you are in a relationship?"

Conryu stared for a moment as he tried to process the question. Why would anyone think he was in a relationship with Heather?

"No," he said.

"Come on," Amanda said. "We've all heard the whispers. Two of the most famous wizards on the planet on the same team. You can't tell me honestly there were no sparks."

"Conryu and I are teammates, nothing more," Heather said.

"If that's the way you want to play it, I don't mind." Amanda sat back down.

The press conference didn't last long after that exchange.

Conryu's answers went from short to monosyllable. Angus bloviated at every opportunity, but the press didn't seem overly interested in him. When the gathering started to break up, Heather tugged on his sleeve.

"Let's go out the back way," she said.

Conryu shrugged, nodded goodbye to Mr. Kane, and followed her past the elevators and to a side entrance he hadn't even known existed. Once they were outside a cool breeze blew over him and drew a sigh. "I'm glad that's over."

Prime flew higher to keep watch. After all the trouble he'd had over the last two years, the scholomantic took his role as lookout seriously, at least when he wasn't in a daze from having so many people around.

"You handled yourself well," Heather said. "I was impressed."

"Thanks, though dealing with the press isn't something I'm interested in getting better at."

"Master, someone's watching us."

Conryu turned straight into a kiss from Heather.

He flailed for a moment then pushed her away. "What the hell was that?"

"Marketing." She licked her lips.

"Are you insane?" Conryu wiped the moisture off his face.

"The spy is gone, Master."

"Not spy, photographer," Heather said. "That image will be on every magazine, newspaper, and news cast."

Conryu considered sending Kai after him, but the risks of a dead photographer were too high. "Why?"

"I told you, marketing. Don't you read the gossip magazines? People eat this sort of thing up. Every time a new movie starts filming, what's the first rumor you hear?" She answered for him. "The leading lady and her costar are having an affair.

It drums up interest. Just enjoy it. Millions of men would give anything to be in your position."

"You're nuts. Stay away from me. Come on, Prime." He needed to get home and tell Maria what happened before she saw it on the news.

* * *

Father Salvador stood in the front of the witch's boat and let the sea spray hit him in the face. Little was visible on the moonless night. He didn't ask Lady Tiger how she saw where they were going, the less he knew about her godless magic the happier it made him.

The chill mist mingled with the smell of salt water as they bounced across the waves. Some of his men leaned over the side and hurled their dinners into the water, an offering for any fish following along in their wake. Part of him preferred to think it was the excitement. God knew Salvador himself was nearly bursting with excitement. He'd always served the Archbishop within the Blessed Kingdom, but at last he'd been chosen to lead the battle against the heathens in their own corrupt country.

He glanced at the captain's station and could just make out the masked figure of Lady Tiger where she gripped the wheel and guided them across the sea. If only they could have avoided using the miserable witch to transport them to the Kingdom of the Isles, he would have judged the crusade without fault. Perhaps God took some secret pleasure in making use of one of His enemies to smite others. Salvador liked to think so.

Half an hour later the shoreline of the Kingdom appeared as a dim outline. The boat slowed as Lady Tiger wove a precise path forward. As he understood it, there existed only a narrow corridor through which they could proceed without drawing the attention of the authorities. Despise her he might, but she'd delivered three hundred of his men to the shore so far and none of them had been detected.

She honored her bargain. It was the only trait he'd found to respect in the woman.

A hundred feet from shore she activated the powerful spotlight built into the front of the boat. A dark beach appeared in the night. Salvador had seldom seen a more desolate stretch of land. It was perfect.

The boat stopped fifteen feet short of the beach. "This is as close as I can get you," Lady Tiger said. "The water's about four feet deep so anything you don't want to get wet needs to be kept above that."

Salvador grunted. He didn't like the witch talking to him as though he was a child. "Over the side, men. Weapons up."

Splashes followed a moment later. When everyone had gotten in he nodded once at Lady Tiger and joined them.

The cold water drew a gasp and he hated himself for the moment of weakness. He'd taken just two steps when the boat's motor engaged and Lady Tiger reversed course, leaving them in the dark. Damned witch.

A pair of flares burst to life up ahead. Soon enough everyone climbed out of the water and onto the sand.

"The map," he said.

Brother Allen, the younger of the two subordinate priests he brought along to serve as his assistants, pulled the plastic-wrapped, many-times-folded piece of paper from the inner pocket of his shirt.

Salvador snatched the map and unfolded it. A circle marked the secret beach and a mile inland an X marked the rendezvous point. In between lay a thick patch of forest. Good for conceal-ment, but lousy for hiking. Smooth or rough, God would see them through.

"Alright men, let's move out. I want one light on point and another in the middle of the formation."

A chorus of "Yes, Father"s rang out and the soldiers of the Blessed Army sorted themselves into formation. They climbed a steep hill and at the top entered the forest. The scent of ever-green lay over everything.

He smiled. As a child Salvador had often played amidst the spruce near his home. The smile turned into a scowl when he stubbed his toe on a half-buried root.

The squad stumbled along in the dark in what he hoped was the correct direction. Nearly an hour later the first hint of dawn revealed a box truck marked with the name of a local farm, Heaven's Hundred Acres, parked on the side of a rutted dirt road. That was their ride.

Salvador worked his way through his men to the front of the gathering. Two soldiers in black bowed to him.

"Welcome, Father," the elder soldier said. "I'm Sergeant Hyack. I trust you met with no difficulties on your journey."

"No, God was watching over us."

Both soldiers made the sign of the cross before Hyack said, "We should load up and get moving. This road doesn't see much traffic, but some of the locals do travel it."

"Of course." The silent soldier lifted the rear door and Salvador motioned his men inside.

When all his soldiers were aboard Hyack winced and said, "You too, Father. The farmers around here have gotten used to us, but a stranger would attract more attention than we want."

Salvador grimaced, but climbed up in with his men. The door slammed down leaving them in total darkness. A vibration ran through the floor when the motor started up and a few seconds later they were bouncing down the road.

They traveled on for Salvador knew not how long. The ride grew smoother and smoother the farther they went before getting rough again. At last the truck stopped and the door slid up. Fresh air washed over him and Salvador breathed deep. Thirty men contained in a small space made for a rancid stench.

Salvador leapt down from the box and glanced around. They were in some sort of poor industrial area. A group of warehouses faced a dirt yard. Beyond them was a rough-looking neighborhood of rundown businesses and tenements. Hardly an inspiring locale, but from humble beginnings great things rose.

"If you'll follow me, Father," Sergeant Hyack said. "I'll introduce you to the leader of our temporary allies. He calls himself The Guv'nor."

Salvador made an effort to hide his distaste. "The anarchist, yes?"

"Yes, Father. They're a rough crew, but they know the city and have been a huge help. I doubt we'd be as far along in our preparations without them."

"Lead on then."

Salvador followed Sergeant Hyack toward the second warehouse from the left. "We've got an office with a cot ready for you, Father. It isn't much, but should hold you for the time being."

Inside the warehouse the stink of unwashed bodies made the back of the truck seem like a day spa. Salvador ignored the stink and focused on his great task. He would bring this city to its knees and make them all regret interfering in God's work.

"Morning, Guv'nor," Hyack said. "This is our leader, Father Salvador."

Salvador blinked once and returned his focus to where it belonged. The man standing in front of him looked to be in his middle twenties, but piercings and tattoos had so warped his flesh that a definite age was impossible to guess. He wore a leather jacket covered in skull patches and stainless steel spikes, filthy ripped jeans, and biker boots.

The punk offered an insolent nod. "Father, welcome to the party. Better late than never."

"Would you give us a minute, Sergeant?" Salvador asked.

Hyack withdrew leaving him alone with the anarchist. "May I ask you something?"

"Knock yourself out."

"Why are you working with us? I've learned a little about anarchists and teaming up with others isn't your style."

The Guv'nor's smile more resembled a death's head grin. "We're using you, mate. Same as you are us."

Salvador's frown deepened.

"Ah, no need to look so indignant. See, a while back we made a move on the Ministry of Magic, trashed the place real good, we did. In the process a lot of my mates ended up in Kingdom prisons. We no longer have the manpower for a raid like this. We also lost some friends in the Dragon Empire so no more magical toys to play with." The Guv'nor shrugged. "When you offered us more bodies, we jumped at the chance."

"Perhaps I explained myself badly," Salvador said. "I meant what was your goal? What do you hope to accomplish with this attack?"

"Nothing, mate. We just like to watch shit burn."

Salvador shook his head. He was allied with a witch and a lunatic. Surely God worked in mysterious ways.

6

LONDON

onryu, Jonny, and Kelsie were jammed into the back of the Kanes' car while Maria and her parents crowded into the front. Mom had offered to bring a couple of them so it wouldn't be so tight, but Mr. Kane told her not to worry about it since the drive wasn't that far. As far as Conryu was concerned it felt like a cross-country trip. He could barely squeeze his shoulders between Jonny and Kelsie, and Prime was riding on his lap.

They hit a pot hole, jostling them together. Jonny whispered, "I can't believe you kissed Heather James."

"It wasn't my idea. She said it was some kind of publicity stunt. I don't know. Hopefully she took the hint and will keep her distance."

He really hoped she did. When he told Maria what happened she'd been furious, thankfully more at Heather than him. His biggest fear at this point was that if Heather tried anything else, Maria might challenge her to a wizard's duel. And though Maria was strong, she hadn't reached her full power yet. Her odds of beating Heather didn't bear thinking about.

"You'll introduce me, right?" Jonny asked.

Conryu grimaced. Since Jonny found out what happened he hadn't been able to talk about anything else. "If I get the chance. Don't get your hopes up. What happened between us was business for her. Unless she can figure some way it will improve her career, I'm afraid you're out of luck."

"Maybe if you tell her I'm in the military. Some chicks are into that."

"Sure, why not?"

Maria glared at them. "Would you please not talk about that bitch in my presence?"

"Sorry," Conryu said.

"Yeah, my bad." Jonny didn't sound the least contrite, but Maria turned back around.

Ten minutes later the Sentinel City International Airport came into view. Two jumbo jets were in the process of taking off. Hundreds of cars jammed the parking lot, but luckily for them they didn't have to worry about finding a spot. The Department's private plane took off from a separate runway and they could drive right out to it.

Mr. Kane swung around towards the rear of the airport. A sleek black jet with the Department logo on it was already surrounded by cars. Conryu spotted Crystal right away, towering over everyone around her. As they got closer, he picked out the rest of the team as well as Coach Chort and Heather. He didn't recognize anyone else, but assumed they were family and friends. Angus would no doubt make himself known shortly.

Mr. Kane parked and they all got out. Conryu and Jonny unloaded luggage while Mr. Kane went to talk to Malice who had emerged from another car. He didn't know what they were discussing and didn't care. As long as Conryu didn't have to deal with her he was happy.

"Dude, I've never flown in a plane before," Johnny said. "We're starting paratrooper training next year so this will be good practice."

"I hope not," Conryu said. "Paratroopers jump out of planes. Where are we supposed to put the suitcases?"

Two men in red security officer uniforms came over and grabbed two bags each. They carried the luggage over to the plane and loaded it into a compartment in the belly. Conryu and Jonny followed along with the rest and tossed them in the nearly full compartment. When they got to the car Mr. Kane had finished his conversation with Malice.

"Looks like we arrived last," Mr. Kane said.

Conryu looked around but didn't see Sonja. Before he could ask Crystal where the little fire wizard was, a portal opened.

Sonja emerged, a suitcase that looked far too big for her clutched in both hands. She looked around at everyone staring at her. "Am I late?"

Conryu grinned. "You're right on time."

Sonja dropped her bag as he approached and hugged him. "Long time no see."

"Likewise." When she let go, he grabbed her bag and carried it over to the plane. He loaded it into the compartment, nodded to the guards, and said, "Last one, fellas."

The men in red set to work getting the compartment closed up and sealed. As Conryu and Sonja walked back to join Johnny and Kelsie she asked, "Done anything exciting lately?"

"I played bodyguard for a while last year." Probably best not to tell her about the war, or the elf artifacts he recovered.

"What about you, anything interesting at the new job?"

"Nothing I can talk about. My project is a super-secret military contract."

"Cool."

Mr. Kane waved at them and pointed toward a staircase on wheels that was slowly approaching the plane. Everyone was walking that way and he'd been too distracted to notice. Conryu nodded and they joined the flow. They fell in at the rear of the line to wait their turn.

"How's the Blinky Mobile?" Sonja asked. "Been driving it much?"

"You know, I didn't have a chance to drive it all year. In fact, I'm not even sure where it is."

They moved a few steps closer. "It didn't get melted down, did it?"

"I don't think so. Most likely it's in storage somewhere."

They reached the top of the stairs and stepped into the cabin. An aisle ran down the center with two seats on either side. Conryu settled in the empty seat beside Maria while Sonja hurried over to hug Crystal. The two girls set to chattering.

"So she was your third guest?" Maria asked.

"Yeah, didn't I tell you?"

"It must've slipped your mind," Maria said. "Maybe you were too busy with Heather."

"Come on, I explained that. I thought you said you weren't mad at me."

"I said I wasn't *that* mad at you, not that I wasn't mad at all."

Sonja dropped into her chair, and a voice came on over the loudspeaker. "Everyone please buckle up, we will be taking off in a moment."

Conryu clicked his seatbelt and sent a silent thank you to the pilot. Perhaps Maria would be less mad when they landed.

* * *

After nearly eight hours on a plane, Conryu realized how much he loved traveling by portal. He could be anywhere in the world in seconds, rather than having his legs fall asleep. Out the window, the sprawling metropolis of London covered everything for miles. He couldn't say for certain, but he would've sworn it looked even bigger than Central.

Maria dozed with her head on his shoulder. Conryu smiled for a moment. She looked so peaceful he hated to wake her. He gave her a nudge.

She groaned and blinked. "What is it?"

"We're here."

"Where?"

"London, remember?"

"Sure." She rubbed sleep from her eyes and leaned across him to peer out the window. "Wow. It's huge. How many people do you suppose live here?"

"About twenty-five million," Mr. Kane said. "It's half again as big as Sentinel City."

"Will we have a chance to look around?" Maria asked.

"We should be able to take in a few sights between matches," Mr. Kane said. "Conryu is going to have to sit the sightseeing out though. The teams are kept under close guard."

Conryu sighed. So much for having a little fun. "Just like the gladiators in Ancient Rome. They're probably afraid we'll try to escape."

The pilot's voice came over the loudspeaker. "Everyone please buckle up. We're coming in for a landing."

Conryu clicked his belt just as the plane banked to make its final approach. The buildings grew ever larger as they flew lower. London's airport had nine runways and they landed at the one farthest from the terminal.

The plane jerked when they hit the tarmac and the tires squealed. The roar of the engines grew quieter as they powered down. When they came to a full stop, the flight attendant opened the door. Everyone started unbuckling and Malice made her way to the exit first.

At the bottom of the stairs, two women waited in flowing red robes marked with crown patches on the shoulders. Behind them a bus with tinted windows sat idling.

The women greeted Malice with bows of respect. The older of the two, assuming the gray streaks in her hair were any indication, said, "Welcome to London, Director Kincaid."

Malice nodded. "Let's keep the meet and greet short. I'd like to get settled in."

"Of course. It'll take a few minutes to transfer your luggage to the bus, but if you'd like to wait on board the air conditioning is running and I think you'll find the seats quite comfortable."

"I'll take you up on that offer." She nodded her withered head again and hobbled off toward the bus, her two toadies falling in behind her.

As soon as she was out of sight the atmosphere lightened and everyone appeared more relaxed. Mr. Kane and the younger woman shook hands. "It's good to see you again, Jemma."

"Likewise, Orin. I believe I owe you a scotch as thanks for getting the password from Ms. Kazakov. Though as it turned out less than three months after we got it decoded the Empire collapsed. All that effort and the data is useless."

Mr. Kane shrugged. "Fortunes of war I guess. Conryu, come meet the London Ministry Chief. Jemma, this is Conryu Koda, he was generous enough to act as Anya's bodyguard."

They shook hands and he was surprised to notice she had a firm grip and calluses. "Mr. Koda, the Ministry owes you a debt as well. If there's anything we can do to make your time in London more pleasant, don't hesitate to ask."

"Thanks. I can't believe I'm about to say this, but I agree with Malice. After eight hours on a plane all I want is a hot shower and something to eat."

Jemma laughed and looked over her shoulder. "Looks like they're almost done transferring the luggage. Once everyone's on board, we can be on our way."

* * *

The bus pulled up to a fancy hotel and stopped. On the sign outside it said, "The Grand Regent." The brakes hissed and the door slid open. Conryu climbed down the steps and stared up at the building. Gilded pillars supported a red velvet canopy and a matching rug ran up to a revolving door. Two doormen in fancy uniforms greeted them as they approached.

"I think this place is even more swanky than your family's hotel in Central," Conryu said.

Kelsie nodded but didn't say anything. She'd been awfully quiet for the whole trip. Having her grandmother nearby probably made her uncomfortable. He tried to think of something he could do to make her feel better, but nothing came to mind. Maybe once Malice left to do official things, whatever those happened to be, she'd be able to relax.

Conryu pushed through the revolving door and found that the inside of the hotel was every bit as elaborate as the outside. Polished, gilded hardwood covered every surface. The lobby was empty except for a few workers behind the check-in desk.

Jemma made her way to the front of the gathering and raised her hands for quiet. "Okay everyone, Alliance team members and coaches please step to the left, everyone else please keep to the right. All team members will be staying on the top floor. Guests will be staying on the two floors below them. If you line up at the desk, you can collect your keys and head upstairs. Feel free to order anything you'd like from room service. Your luggage will be brought up shortly. Thank you."

Coach Chort herded everyone towards the desk and Conryu lined up behind Crystal. When his turn came a pretty blond in a red-and-gold uniform handed him a piece of plastic that resembled a credit card. It had the number four on it.

He glanced at Crystal. "What room did you get?"

Crystal held up her card. "Seven, what about you?"

"I got four. What do you suppose the rooms will be like?"

"Nice."

He grinned. Conryu had no doubt she was right about that.

When the last girl had collected her keys, they all fell in behind Jemma who guided them to the elevators. Conryu waved at Maria and Kelsie before he climbed into the car. They rode up to the twentieth floor and stepped out into the hall. Six young men in red-and-black uniforms stood at attention.

"These cadets will be serving as your personal bodyguards," Jemma said. "Their duty is to keep you safe."

Conryu eyed the cadets. None of them looked older than he was. They probably had at least as good a training as

Jonny, but he wouldn't want to depend on any of them in a real fight. He suspected their main function was ceremonial.

They paired off and he ended up with a young man named Grant.

"It's an honor to be protecting you, sir," Grant said.

"Don't kid me," Conryu said. "You drew the short straw getting stuck with me, right?"

Grant quirked an eyebrow. "I don't know what you mean, sir."

Conryu stepped into his room and Grant followed. "Come on. There are five nice-looking girls on the team plus me. You telling me getting stuck protecting the only guy in the tournament isn't bad luck?"

When he closed the door Grant sighed. "We didn't draw straws. We put each of your names in a hat and everyone drew one. I went first and still got you. No offense."

"None taken. I wouldn't have wanted to protect me either in your position. Did they even tell you how many people have tried to kill me over the years?"

"No, sir."

"Probably just as well. I'm not sure how I feel about having someone with such bad luck watching my back."

"I may not be the luckiest person in the world, but I know how to fight."

"Good. So what now, you sleep outside my door?" Conryu asked.

Grant barked a laugh. It was the first break in his stony expression Conryu had seen. "Hardly. They've got us all jammed into two rooms nearby. We're only responsible for you during the day when you're out and about. At night you're on your own."

"That's good to know. Now go away. I am going to take a shower."

Grant laughed and ducked out the door. Seemed like a nice enough guy, but Kai wasn't in any danger of losing her job.

* * *

Conryu sighed and pushed the room service cart out into the hall. After the bellhop finally brought his suitcase, he changed into his pajamas and ordered dinner. They were on their own until nine the next morning and he intended to enjoy his downtime.

The food at the hotel was every bit as nice as the decor. He hadn't had a steak that tender in a long time. The only problem was they didn't serve pizza, not that it would've compared to Giovanni's anyway. Oh well, he'd have something to look forward to when he got home.

He tossed aside the covers and ran his fingers along the soft sheets. They made the bedding at the Academy feel like sandpaper. He needed to be careful not to get too used to the luxury since he'd probably never have another chance to enjoy a place like this.

"Prime, you ready?"

"Yes, Master."

Something must be wrong; the scholomantic hadn't issued a complaint all day. Not that he intended to complain. It was probably having so many people around that made Prime uncomfortable. He'd complained about it before after all.

Conryu checked his phone one last time, flipped off the light, and slid between the sheets. It'd been a long day and he intended to sleep well tonight.

He'd started to doze, when a creak came from the door.

There was a flash of light from the hall that quickly vanished. Who could be visiting him at this time of night? He doubted it would be Maria or Kelsie, they'd both looked exhausted when they got off the plane. Besides, they'd have knocked. Conryu frowned. He'd locked the door, he was sure of it.

Well whoever they were, he had a nasty surprise for them. He focused his will and released a light spell. He closed his eyes an instant before the spell burst, and when he opened them he found Heather James standing there in a thin red silk robe blinking and peering around.

"What do you want now?" he asked.

She rubbed her eyes one last time and finally focused on him. "I wanted to apologize. I didn't think you'd be so upset about that little kiss."

"Little kiss? You examined my tonsils with your tongue."

"I may have got a little carried away." She came closer to the bed, giving him a good look at her long legs. "Like I said, I wanted to say I was sorry."

"Apology accepted." He needed to get her out of his room. Like, yesterday. "Anything else?"

She loosed the tie at the front of her robe and let it hang open. "I thought I'd try to make it up to you."

She shrugged and the robe fell to the floor. Heather James in all her naked glory was a sight to behold. Any questions he may have had—and he didn't have many — about why pretty much everyone considered her the most beautiful woman in the world were answered in that moment.

"No cameras, no reporters." She climbed on the foot of the bed and slid toward him. "Just you and me."

"Stop! Just stop. I got mad at you for kissing me and you imagine this is the way to make me feel better?"

She froze halfway to him and stared as if not entirely certain what he was saying. "You're turning me down?"

The incredulity in her voice almost made him laugh. "Yes. Now get your robe and go away."

She knelt in the middle of his bed, seeming unable to move. "No one's ever turned me down before."

That he believed. "Well, there's a first time for everything."

She sniffed and a tear ran down her face. "You don't understand. If we don't do this I stand to lose everything."

Now it was Conryu's turn to be confused. "Maybe you'd better explain."

She broke down in sobs, her whole body shaking. Since she didn't have any clothes on it was very distracting. Conryu got out of bed, grabbed her robe, and slung it around her shoulders.

When she got herself under control, Heather said, "It's Malice. She wants your genetic material and told me if I didn't get it she'd arrange for me to lose my modeling contract."

"So that's the real reason you joined the team?" It certainly made more sense than having her advise them about combat strategy.

"It's not the only reason, but it is part of it. The Department did think having me on the team would improve the ratings. When Malice found out, she made her threat."

Conryu massaged the bridge of his nose. "Even if we did what you wanted, how would you collect the... sample?"

Heather wiped a tear off her cheek. "She implanted a device in me before I came here. It will collect the sample and keep it secure. I'm sorry, I didn't know what else to do."

She started crying again and Conryu found he felt bad for her. Malice seemed to have a knack for ruining the lives of everyone around her, first Kelsie and now Heather. He sat beside her and squeezed her arm. "Couldn't you just tell her you tried, but it didn't work?"

"I don't think she'd go for that. Either I succeeded or I failed, there are no excuses with her."

Heather lunged at him, wrapped her arms around his neck, and kissed him again.

Conryu pulled away and sent her sprawling on the floor. "And here I was starting to feel bad for you. Get dressed and get out. You and Malice deserve each other."

She got to her feet and glared at him, still naked. Conryu glared right back, so angry he was able to overlook her body.

He pointed at the door. "Now!"

"What if I say no?"

"Then I'll throw you into the hall naked."

For a moment he feared she might actually make him do it, then she shrugged into her robe and stomped over to the door. "This isn't over."

She slammed the door behind her as she left.

When she'd gone, Conryu turned to Prime. "How about a little warning next time?"

"Sorry, Master. I was asleep and by the time I realized someone was there you'd already dealt with her."

"You've been in one of those trances like when we were hunting Lady Raven?"

"Yes. So many people, Master. If I maintain full awareness, I'm on the verge of biting someone every moment."

"Just remember I count on you to warn me about this sort of thing. If you're not on your game, I'm more vulnerable."

"Understood, Master. I'll try to do better."

"Good."

At least Kai hadn't appeared and accidentally killed her. That would have been really hard to explain. This time, before

Conryu went to sleep, he placed a dark ward in front of the door. If anyone else was stupid enough to sneak in, they'd regret it.

* * *

At night on the London streets, even in the bad part of the city, it never got truly dark. Lady Tiger appreciated that fact as she stepped over a puddle that stank far worse than water had a right to. This wretched alley served as a miserable counterpoint to the opulent gathering she'd left only hours ago.

She'd been invited as Lady Tish to attend a cocktail party with the other wealthy donors who were helping fund the elf artifact exhibit. Wealthy idiots that wouldn't know a relic if someone shoved it up their nose. The whole affair was simply an excuse to put on their most expensive gowns and jewels and preen for their peers. She hated that sort of thing, but Lady Tish was expected to attend so she did. Anything that brought her cover into question needed to be avoided until she'd secured the artifact fragment. After that they could all burn.

The alley opened up into a large industrial area full of rundown warehouses. It didn't look like this part of the city had seen much of the economic revival the government had been boasting about.

Lady Tiger looked from one dilapidated building to the next. Not the most inspiring base of operations, but what could you expect when dealing with anarchists and madmen? She turned left and strode over to the second building. The priest, Father Salvador, said the building served as their command center. No sound escaped the walls and no light filtered out through the filthy windows. At least they were doing a good job not advertising their presence.

Ignoring the large main entrance, she went to a side door and knocked.

After a short wait the door opened and an unshaven face appeared in the gap. "What the bloody hell do you want?" he asked.

"I'm an acquaintance of the priest. He's expecting me."

The filthy little man eyed her for a moment before slamming the door in her face. She grimaced at the rude treatment. Under other circumstances she'd have been delighted to teach him proper manners, but these weren't normal circumstances.

After a nearly five-minute wait, the door opened again, this time all the way. Father Salvador stood just inside in his black uniform. The lines of his face had deepened and his hard, suspicious eyes burned with excitement.

"I wouldn't have your foul presence corrupt this holy place on the night before battle, but the Archbishop commands us to work with you and we obey. Come inside before you're seen."

She stepped through the door and into the warehouse. Instantly, the overwhelming stench of gasoline mixed with too many unwashed bodies nearly made her gag. Thank goodness her mask hid her revulsion. He called this rat hole a holy place? The priest was madder than she'd thought.

A large group of men worked on various projects throughout the space. Many of the weapons they had she recognized, plenty she didn't. Wizards had no need for such crude items. With a thought she activated a magic-detection spell. A few items glowed, but nothing of real power revealed itself.

Lady Tiger turned to the priest. "It seems your preparations are coming along well."

"When the time comes, we will be ready to do our part. For the glory of God we will send the wizard lovers to Hell."

She grimaced behind her mask. He really was a lunatic. They strode together through the gathered warriors, if you wanted to call them that. The powers that be would designate them terrorists. Most looked at her with suspicion if not outright hatred. She paused in front of one man who was gently stroking a ball that looked like it was made of leather. The sphere gave off one of the more potent auras she'd seen.

"What is that?" she asked.

"A last gift from a fallen ally." The man giggled and stared at her with bright, insane eyes.

That told her little, but she doubted the man had the wherewithal to elaborate. Leaving the lunatic behind they continued their inspection. Thirty men toiled at a long table, making improvised bombs, loading clips, and polishing weapons. The guns and knives were the only clean things she'd seen since entering the building.

When they reached the far side of the space Father Salvador said, "Each building contains a group like this. My holy soldiers have allied with the anarchists and together we'll burn this wretched city to the ground."

Lady Tiger seriously doubted that, but she only nodded. Once she got the artifact, they could do whatever they wanted. She intended to be long gone by then.

7

OPENING CEREMONY

After Heather's visit, Conryu had a hard time getting back to sleep. It wasn't that he expected her to return and try again, more that he couldn't get his heart to stop hammering a thousand miles an hour. He loved Maria, more than anything, but he was only human and Heather, whatever else you might say about her, was a stunning woman.

At the same time, he couldn't remember the last time he'd been so angry. At both her and Malice. What was he going to have to do to get the Kincade family to leave him alone? Conryu didn't want to make threats, especially since he probably wasn't willing to do anything really violent to them anyway.

God! What had she been thinking? How much of her story was true? She'd sounded sincere, but he didn't trust himself to judge. One thing was certain, it was going to be awkward at the opening ceremony today.

He tried to meditate and empty his mind. He couldn't

control what might happen later so he needed to let it go. What would be, would be, as Dad liked to say.

Conryu jumped out of bed and took a cold shower in hopes that it would wake him up. Fifteen minutes later he was dressed and ready to go downstairs to the hotel restaurant. Conryu was supposed to meet Kelsie, Jonny and the Kanes for breakfast. He still hadn't made up his mind whether he should tell Maria about what happened. Part of him understood he had to, but he didn't want to risk her doing anything crazy. For someone so generally in control, she had a quick temper sometimes.

He almost laughed out loud. Imagine him worrying about Maria doing something rash. He sighed. There was no way around it, he was going to have to tell her. If she found out some other way, she'd never trust him again. He didn't dare take that chance.

Conryu opened the door and found Grant standing in the hall in a crisp uniform, hands clasped behind his back, waiting for him. A quick glance down the hall revealed the other cadets waiting for their charges to emerge.

"Did you sleep well, sir?" Grant asked.

"Not as well as I would've liked. Are you planning to follow me down to breakfast?"

"It's my job to follow you wherever you go, sir. Please don't try to ditch me, if you do I'll catch hell over it with my commander."

Perhaps Grant could help him restrain Maria when he told her what Heather had done. "Well let's get a move on then."

As he rode down the elevator Conryu asked, "Am I the first one up?"

"Yes, sir. I suspect the others will join you shortly. The bus is due to arrive in an hour and a half to pick everyone up."

The elevator bell chimed and the door slid open. Conryu stepped out into the lobby and looked around, trying to spot the others. He didn't see anyone, but they might've been waiting in the restaurant already.

"Prime, do you sense Maria anywhere?"

"No, Master."

Guess he'd just have to look around. He walked across the lobby to the restaurant. The maître d', a skinny little man with a long, pointy nose and oiled, slicked-back hair, intercepted him as he tried to enter. "Do you have a reservation, sir?"

"I'm meeting some friends for breakfast. My name is Conryu Koda, I'm on the North American Alliance team."

The maître d's eyes widened. "I'm so sorry, sir, I didn't recognize you without your robe. Two members of your party arrived just minutes ago. I'll take you to them."

Conryu and Grant followed the little man deeper into the restaurant. He spotted Kelsie and Jonny seated together at a long table. Grant took up position at a small table nearby, close enough to act if he needed to, but far enough away to give them some privacy.

"Dude, this place is awesome." Jonny glanced at Grant. "Who's the stiff?"

"My bodyguard."

Jonny laughed. "They gave *you* a bodyguard?"

"It wasn't my idea," Conryu said. "How are you holding up, Kelsie? You haven't had any run-ins with your grandmother, have you?"

"No, thank goodness. Grandmother seems intent on avoiding me and I'm happy to follow her lead. I shouldn't be afraid of her, it's not like the family can take anything else away from me."

"No, but being cautious with her isn't a terrible idea."

Conryu felt bad for her. Before the Kincades tried to get Heather to sleep with him, they gave the job to Kelsie. She was entirely too sweet to make much of an effort. And thank goodness for that. If she'd tried what Heather did, he didn't know if he'd ever be able to look at her again.

He took a moment to center himself and banish the negative thoughts. If he never had to see Malice again, it would suit him just fine. Unfortunately, he doubted he was going to be so lucky.

Conryu took the chair beside Kelsie and when the waiter came over to check on him ordered an orange juice. The young lady hadn't even returned with his drink when Maria and her parents entered the restaurant.

Conryu got to his feet, pulled out the chair beside him for Maria, and whispered in her ear, "We need to talk after."

She gave him a quizzical look, but he just shook his head. What he had to tell her shouldn't be said in front of others. Mr. and Mrs. Kane sat beside Johnny across from them.

"Nervous, Conryu?" Mrs. Kane asked.

"No, but everyone seems to think I should be. So what about you guys? What do you have to do during the opening ceremony?"

"Nothing important," Mr. Kane said. "We'll be sitting with the director and watching the event on a monitor. We'll be in the same room as the other nations' representatives so politics will certainly be discussed."

"I think I'd rather fight a demon than sit beside Malice for half a day talking about politics," Conryu said.

Mr. Kane chuckled. "She can be a little hard to take, but Malice gets things done. I may not always agree with her, but then who always agrees with their boss?"

They enjoyed a quiet breakfast, but when it was over he had

to bite the bullet. Conryu got up and held out his hand to Maria. She took it and he led her out to the lobby. When Grant started to get up, Conryu shook his head. He did not need an audience for what was coming.

They found a set of chairs in an out-of-the-way corner and sat facing each other. "What's so important?" Maria asked.

Conryu took a breath and tried to release some of his tension. "Heather came to see me last night. Malice hired her to collect my genetic material."

Maria's hands clenched and relaxed like she wanted to strangle someone. "And how did she propose to go about doing that?"

"How do you think?"

"Did she succeed?"

Conryu shook his head, a little hurt. "Do you really need to ask?"

"No, sorry. Just so you know, I'm going to have to kill her."

She said it so calmly, but from the look in her eye he knew she meant it. "I can't believe I'm about to say this, but please don't do anything rash." Conryu took her hands in his. "I'm afraid you're not strong enough to win a duel against her. Maybe when you finish school, but not now."

"You really think I can't beat her?" Maria asked.

"Right now you're only at fifty percent of your maximum potential. She's already reached hers plus she has four more years of experience. If it came to a fight, I'm afraid you'd lose and lose badly. I know you don't want to hear it, but it's the truth."

Maria's jaw clenched, and he feared for a moment she might continue to argue. Instead, she made a deliberate effort to calm down. "Alright, I won't kill the bitch now, but she is going to pay for this. I promise you."

Conryu suspected Maria was right. When Malice found out she failed, the confrontation would not be pleasant. For a moment, a teeny part of him actually felt bad for Heather. But only for a moment.

* * *

An hour and a half after breakfast, the same tour bus that brought them from the airport to the hotel arrived to take them to the stadium. Maria had gotten herself fully under control, for which Conryu was grateful. The team, guests, and everyone else going to the tournament stood waiting under the canopy outside the hotel. Malice came hobbling outside, the last to arrive. For a moment Conryu thought she gave him an extra-close look, but he probably just imagined it.

The bus door opened and the old witch boarded first. Heather wouldn't even meet his gaze when he looked her way. Perhaps she had a little bit of shame in her.

He climbed up the steps and joined the rest of his team at the rear of the bus. When he'd taken his seat, Coach Chort leaned forward and said, "The real test starts now. All your training was for this moment. I have faith in you."

Not the most inspiring pre-fight speech, but she seemed sincere. Conryu expected some sort of discussion about tactics or maybe just about what sort of events they could expect today. Coach seemed content to simply lean back and close her eyes. It seemed she was confident she'd done as much as she could.

He followed her example and closed his eyes. Queen's Stadium was only a mile from the hotel—even with London traffic it shouldn't take them that long to make the trip. After only a few seconds, it became clear to him that he wouldn't be able to relax. He shifted his focus to the link with Prime. The scholomantic's thoughts seemed sluggish this morning. He'd probably gone into hibernation mode.

Conryu gave him a mental prod. Annoyance came through their link, but Prime opened his eyes. He strengthened their connection and looked around at his teammates. Everyone smiled and high-fived, ready, even eager, for the tournament to get underway.

For his part, Conryu just wanted the whole thing over with. In a few days, he'd be home and free to enjoy the rest of his summer vacation. He focused on that until they reached the stadium and the brakes hissed, announcing their arrival.

He looked out his window, but was on the wrong side to see the stadium. Everyone stood up and started piling out of the bus. At the bottom of the steps, he stared up at Queen Stadium for the first time. It made Sentinel Stadium look like a minor league ballpark. The designers had made it to resemble the Roman Coliseum, only built on a massive scale and with a dome covering it. He tried to imagine how many people it could hold and failed.

The Ministry wizard, Jemma, along with two others in matching red robes emerged from the stadium and made their way over.

"Hello, again," Jemma said. "I hope everyone slept well. If the Alliance team will follow me, my assistants will get the rest of you settled."

"Good luck," Maria said.

Jonny and Conryu bumped fists. Kelsie glanced at her grandmother then gave him an encouraging nod and smile.

He joined his teammates and followed Jemma to the left away from the main entrance. They walked for the better part of a block before reaching a ramp that led to a tunnel. A little ways down the tunnel, three other groups in robes stood waiting.

"We were the last to arrive?" Conryu asked.

"Yes, please join the others. We'll call you out to the field in about fifteen minutes." Jemma made a shooing motion toward the tunnel and retraced her steps back the way she'd come.

The team went down to the end of the passage and stopped directly across from a group of six tall blond girls. He would've bet his bike that was the Australian Republic's team. The two groups eyed each other for a few seconds before the blond girl in black robes stepped out from the line.

She held out her hand to Conryu. "I'm Dot, I've read all about you. To be honest, I thought you'd be taller."

Conryu gave her hand a shake. "Nice to meet you. Were you on last year's team?"

She shook her head. "Missed it by a whisker."

"I guess we're both rookies then. Good luck."

"You too."

"They'll need it," the light magic wizard from the Empire of the Rising Sun said. "Maybe with the new lineup you'll finish better than last, but I doubt it."

Heather glared but Coach Chort cut things off before they could escalate. "All right, enough jawing."

The Empire's coach said something harsh in Imperial Japanese, and the light magic wizard lowered her head. Conryu spoke a little of the language, but that wasn't a phrase he was familiar with.

When her coach looked away, the Imperial wizard gave them one last sneer of disdain before returning her attention to the rest of her team. Considering they were all supposed to be allies, there didn't seem to be much camaraderie. He guessed it was foolish to expect much when national pride was on the line.

Jemma's voice came on over the PA system. "Ladies and gentlemen, we are here today to begin the Four Nations Tournament. For over a century, this tournament has been a way for the four nations to forge closer relationships and have a good time. I trust this year will be no exception. Instead of our usual four, however, we have a fifth joining us."

"What's the meaning of this?" the coach of the Imperial team asked in English.

Conryu hadn't heard anything about an extra team. It was probably just another trick to drum up an audience.

"Our new ally, France, has sent their first ever representative team to join us. Please offer them a warm welcome."

A song started playing and everyone moved closer to the end of the tunnel. Six girls emerged from a tunnel on the opposite side and trotted out onto the huge field. They all wore robes appropriate to their alignment, and each had a Fleur-de-Lis on her shoulder.

Conryu didn't even know France had a magic school and now they had a team. Well, these were the sorts of surprises you ran into when you didn't pay attention to the goings on in the wizard world.

The French team stopped at the center of the field and waved at the empty stadium, or more accurately the cameras that would show every move they made.

"Next we welcome the Empire of the Rising Sun's team and the defending tournament champions."

A different song started playing and the girls and their coach marched out onto the field. When they had taken their place beside the French team, the Kingdom team was announced. Next came the Australian team, and finally the Alliance team marched out to their national anthem.

Conryu looked all around, staring in awe at the huge empty stadium. They were expected to compete without a single person watching? That would be so weird. Come to think of it, he remembered when he watched the tournament at home that they didn't allow anyone to be present lest they get hurt by an out-of-control spell. This was certainly going to take a little getting used to.

"And there they are," Jemma said. "Without further ado, let the tournament begin."

* * *

Malice eased herself down to the chair in the front row of the skybox. The walk up had been pure hell on her old bones, but with grim determination she made it without a word of complaint. A huge window dominated the front of the luxury seating area. Down on the field the teams had separated themselves and were preparing for the first round of team casting. Malice wasn't overly interested in watching as she already had a fairly good idea how it was going to turn out.

"Are you comfortable, Aunt Malice?" one of her aides asked.

"That's Director Malice and I'm fine. Now be quiet." Behind her people shifted as they found their seats. The skybox held fifty people so there was plenty of room for everyone.

Though the match didn't much interest her, what did was trying to figure out how Heather had failed to seduce Conryu. Malice was no expert in such matters, but considering the approach Heather took it seemed that she should have succeeded.

Malice ground her teeth. What was it going to take to get

what she needed? After Heather's failure, Malice found she actually felt a bit of sympathy for Kelsie. Clearly the boy wasn't just another ignorant, undisciplined man. That would make her task more complicated, but she would figure it out.

Down on the field, Conryu blew away the Australian team's construct with a blast of dark magic bigger than anything she'd ever seen. Such displays only made her more determined. She would get the boy's genetic material no matter what it took.

"What a showoff."

Malice looked over her shoulder to see who spoke. It was Chief Kane's daughter. According to Kelsie, she and Conryu were dating.

Understanding slowly dawned on Malice. As long as the boy was in a relationship with someone else, they had no hope of success. He was simply too honorable to betray someone he cared about. Malice turned back to the window, a slow, evil smile spreading across her face, one that would have frozen the blood of anyone seeing it.

She finally knew what she had to do. The Kane girl needed to be eliminated. Once that was done, Conryu was sure to turn to Kelsie for comfort. Once that happened, nature would take its course and she would finally get what she wanted. And if she was honest with herself, so would her granddaughter.

The only question was, how best to get rid of the girl. It would have to look like an accident. There could be no sign of Kincade involvement. If Conryu had any idea she was involved, Malice hated to think what he might be capable of.

Yes, discretion was definitely the way to go.

* * *

Lady Tiger parked her red luxury sports car across from the Museum of Magic. It was ten o'clock and the traffic in this part of the city was minimal. She paused before she got out, making a mental note of the spells she'd need. Tonight was the night, soon the artifact would be hers. When the Blessed Army attacked the next day, the Ministry would be too busy dealing with them to chase her. By the time the fools figured out the theft was the bigger threat it would be too late.

She got out and leaned on the roof, the cool metal feeling good against her bare arms. Across the street, all the lights were out save for those on the top floor. The smug society matrons would be in for a show tonight. She patted the car with a black-gloved hand. Over the past few days she'd gotten used to driving the powerful car and found it oddly exhilarating. It was the only thing she'd miss when she abandoned the Lady Tish persona.

A quick glance revealed no vehicles in her vicinity so she crossed the street and walked up to the museum doors. A security guard in a blue uniform looked at her through the glass door. Lady Tiger pulled her invitation from her purse and held it up.

The guard nodded, unlocked the door, and opened it for her. "Good evening, ma'am. Enjoy the party."

She strode through, completely ignoring him. The elevators waited at the rear of the lobby. She got into the first one and rode it up to the top floor. The elevator chimed and the door slid open.

Thirteen pedestals had been erected in the large empty space. Each pedestal held a single elf artifact. Her gaze was drawn at once to the broken semicircle that was a twin to the piece Lady Wolf had already acquired.

"Dear Lady Tish." Ms. Pollock came striding up to her, hands extended in greeting. Lady Tiger steeled herself and took the approaching noblewoman's fingers in a gentle grip. They exchanged kisses on the cheek. "You're a bit late, dear. I was afraid you might not make it."

"Fashionable, I believe is the word. Never fear," Lady Tiger said. "I wouldn't miss tonight for the world."

"It's quite exciting, isn't it?" Ms. Pollock gestured at the gathered rich and famous. "The interest was greater than I expected. I don't know what it is about magic, but it always seems to draw people's curiosity. Though I must admit, I'd hoped the artifacts would be more showy."

Lady Tiger restrained a grimace at the woman's ignorance. As they walked around the room and Ms. Pollock introduced her to this or that famous personage, she noticed a number of people dressed in red robes standing unobtrusively here and there around the room. When they finally had a moment of peace Lady Tiger asked, "What's with the wizards?"

"Ugh, the Ministry insisted that their guards remain here at all times. Tacky, I know. If they can't trust the cream of the Kingdom's wealthy, who can they trust? I tried to convince them that having guards would ruin the atmosphere, but they made it clear that if we wanted the artifacts, the guards were nonnegotiable."

Lady Tiger made soothing noises while inside she seethed. So far she counted ten Ministry wizards and that only included the ones inside, there had to be more outside patrolling the skies above the museum. There was no way she was going to be able to steal the artifact with that many wizards keeping watch.

Silently cursing the Ministry's efficiency, she went through the motions of chatting with her so-called peers. After an hour of schmoozing she couldn't take any more.

"I fear, Ms. Pollock, that my stomach is in a foul mood tonight. I'm afraid I shall have to retire early, but please believe me when I say I had a lovely evening."

Ms. Pollock patted her on the hand. "I'm sorry to see you go, dear, but sometimes you get bad hors d'oeuvres. No help for it, you know. Get some rest and I'm sure tomorrow you'll be right as rain in the morning."

Lady Tiger offered a wan smile. "You're very kind. Good evening."

She wove her way over to the elevators and rode down, her mind racing as she tried to come up with a new plan. If they kept constant watch over the artifact at the museum, there was no way she could get it there. She crossed the street and dropped into her driver-side bucket seat.

Several deep breaths calmed her racing mind. She hadn't come this far just to fail now. One way or another she would complete her task.

An hour past midnight, a black panel van with the Ministry logo painted on the side pulled up to the front of the museum. Lady Tiger perked up. Maybe this would be the opportunity she was looking for.

Five Ministry wizards leapt out of the van and formed a circle around it. Moments later the wizards from upstairs emerged, each carrying a case. In less than a minute all the wizards as well as the artifacts were in the van and on the move.

Lady Tiger started her car and followed them. She tried her best to keep one or two cars back from the van at all times. Surveillance wasn't her specialty, but as with most wizards, they were more likely to notice a magical attempt to spy on them than someone simply following along behind.

Hopefully.

She followed them through the late-night London traffic for the better part of fifteen minutes. After weaving a circuitous route around the city, they finally pulled into the underground parking lot at the Ministry building. Lady Tiger drove on past as though she was just another partier on her way home after a late night.

Given the time it took to drive from the Ministry to the museum, as well as the time the display opened to the public tomorrow, she knew the wizards would have to leave at about eight thirty in the morning.

Her tires screeched as she slammed on the brakes and pulled across three lanes of traffic. The other drivers honked at her but she paid them no mind. If she could convince Father Salvador to move up his schedule, she might still have a chance.

* * *

The neighborhoods grew poorer and poorer as Lady Tiger grew closer to the warehouses. Soon her car was the only one visible without rust or bullet holes. She suspected that if she wanted it to disappear, all she'd have to do was park it on the side of the road in this area for five minutes.

As she drove she tried to think of an argument that might sway Father Salvador. The priest was dedicated to his mission, so perhaps if she framed her case in terms of improving his odds of success. More likely he'd simply reject anything she had to say out of hand because it came from a wizard. Well, that's what mind control spells were for.

She pulled into the open area in front of the warehouses, got out, slipped her mask in place, and wove a simple protective ward around her car. That would ensure it was still there when she returned.

Lady Tiger marched over to the warehouse door and knocked. It seemed to take forever, but finally the same doorman as the night before appeared. "You again? What do you want now?"

"I need to speak to Father Salvador immediately."

He glowered at her for a moment then slammed the door. If she didn't need every man for the attack, she'd have happily killed the moron where he stood. Instead, that pleasure would belong to someone else.

After what seemed an eternity, he finally returned. "Father says he's got nothing more to say to you. So step off."

"It's very important that I talk to him. Did you make that clear?"

"I told him, and he don't seem interested." The doorman pointed a gun at her. "Now bugger off."

She glared at him and the gun began to glow red hot. He hissed and dropped it.

"My will is your will, my wish your command, Puppet Master!"

His expression went slack and a moment later he said, "How may I serve, Mistress?"

"Take me to the priest."

He opened the door for her and then led her through the warehouse. A few people glanced their way, but most seemed to have fallen asleep, either in ragged cots or on top of heaps of equipment. The grubby man led her to an office at the rear of the warehouse.

"He's in there, Mistress. Be careful. He has a violent temper. Shall I shoot him first, just to be safe?"

"No need." Lady Tiger waved him off.

She tried the knob and found it unlocked.

When she entered Father Salvador looked up from a map of the city. "I thought I made it clear I didn't want to speak to you again."

"You did, but circumstances have changed. I need you to alter your plan of attack. A morning strike would serve you better than a midday battle."

"What makes you think that?"

"With fewer people out you will be able to move around more easily, but still have plenty of targets." Even in her own mind it sounded like a weak argument.

He steepled his fingers and looked at her over the tips. "Fewer people mean fewer heretics to send to their final judgement. We will attack at noon as planned. Leave now while you're still able."

"I had hoped to convince you reasonably, but I can see that is not to be. My will is your will, my wish your command, Puppet Master!"

Her spell ran into a barrier of some sort and fizzled.

He glared at her. "You think I am some weak-willed fool you can control with your godless magic?"

She couldn't believe the spell didn't work. An ordinary man like Salvador should've had no defense against her magic.

He reached into the front of his shirt and pulled out a silver cross. "God's blessing protects me from your evil spells. As long as I have this, no wizard can control me."

With a thought she activated detection magic. As she feared, the cross radiated a protective spell. She doubted the idiot even knew he had on a magic item. Lady Tiger didn't have time to determine exactly what it did, but it was enough to know that protected them from a domination spell.

Father Salvador leapt to his feet. "You betrayed me and the Archbishop, witch. For that you will die tonight."

He reached under the desk and an alarm went off. The sound of boots thumping on wooden floor filled the air. Lady Tiger didn't fear the men or their feeble weapons, but she didn't want to kill them all either. Dead soldiers were of little use.

"You may consider yourself fortunate that your lives are still of value to me." She cast a flight spell and burned her way through the ceiling and out into the night sky.

She landed beside her car, jumped in, and raced away. There was no help to be had with her former allies. Whatever she was going to do, she was going to have to do it on her own.

8

UNDER ATTACK

Conryu rolled over and grabbed his phone. Six thirty, great. Why in the world would they start today's matches so early? If he knew who was in charge of scheduling, Conryu would have happily introduced them to the Reaper. He was still exhausted from yesterday's two matches. You'd think the powers that be would want the wizards at their best.

Oh well, if he was tired all the others would be too so he supposed it was fair. He tossed the covers off and climbed out of bed. At least he got a decent night's sleep with no unexpected visitors dropping in. In fact, he hadn't spoken to Heather since her late-night visit, not even in her official assistant coaching capacity.

"Prime, are you awake?"

"Yes, Master. As you requested, I've been endeavoring to remain more alert."

"Good. I have no idea what Heather might try next, but she doesn't strike me as the sort to just give up."

After a nice hot shower and a bite of breakfast, it was time to head downstairs. The group waiting this morning was way smaller than yesterday. It seemed everyone else had sense enough to sleep in. He spotted Coach Chort and walked over.

"You know why we're getting started so early?" he asked.

Coach shrugged. "No idea. For all I know the tournament committee simply decided it would be fun to see how we performed first thing in the morning. It doesn't really matter, since it's the same for everyone and everything is shown on tape delay. I trust you're feeling up to snuff?"

"Oh I'm fine, though my brain still thinks it's the middle of the night. If I was a suspicious sort, I might think they wanted to give an advantage to the home team."

"That's entirely possible. The Alliance has done similar things when we hosted the tournament. All part of the home-field advantage."

Mr. and Mrs. Kane stepped out of the elevators and headed their way, though there was no sign of Maria. Conryu gave Coach Chort a nod and walked over to talk to them.

"Is Maria not coming?" he asked.

"No, when they heard what time we were going everyone decided to stay in and watch the match on tv," Mr. Kane said.

He didn't blame them for not wanting to get up. If Conryu had his way, he would just as soon stay with his friends. Unfortunately, that wasn't an option for him.

He spotted Crystal a little way off by herself, a worried frown creasing her brow. Curious, he went over. "What's wrong?"

"It's Sonja, she's come down with a cold. Probably caught it on the plane."

"So she's not coming either?"

"No. I offered to heal her. Even though it's not my alignment I can manage well enough to cure a simple cold, but she insisted I save my strength for the match. She assured me she could sleep it off in a day or two so I left her in bed with a glass of orange juice on the nightstand."

"Sonja's tougher than she looks. I bet she'll be up and about in no time."

Crystal nodded, still looking worried.

They waited another ten minutes and loaded up the bus. Neither Malice nor Heather bothered to put in an appearance and he couldn't say he missed either of them. On the other hand, he liked knowing where they were so he didn't worry about what they were getting up to.

The ride over to the stadium was smooth enough and before he knew it they were unloading in the morning fog and making their way to the entry tunnel.

"We're in the first match against the Kingdom team," Coach said. "It starts in a few minutes so everyone get your game faces on."

Conryu yawned and soon everyone was following suit. Yawning soon gave way to sleepy laughter and even Coach Chort cracked a smile. "This is not what I meant by game faces."

A few minutes later, Jemma's voice came over the loudspeaker and called out the Kingdom team. Coach looked them all over and nodded. "Good luck."

"And currently in the middle of the pack, the North American Alliance team," the announcer said. Middle of the pack was certainly better than last year, but if Conryu had to compete in this stupid tournament, he would have liked to be a little higher in the standings, like at the top.

The problem was that despite the fact that he won all his individual challenges easily, the rest of the team only won half of theirs. Conryu was only allowed to participate in full team competitions and dark magic challenges. If teams of one were permitted, he'd be in first place, but that wasn't how the game worked.

They marched out onto the field and stopped ten steps from their opponents. As Conryu had expected the Kingdom team looked well rested and eager to go.

"I'm sure everyone here knows the rules," the announcer said. "But for those watching at home I'll just go over them quickly. Today's match is a group melee that will continue until all members of one team have been knocked unconscious or otherwise made unable to continue. Lethal spells are of course forbidden, so be sure to modulate your attack strength."

The ten-second countdown began and everyone cast defensive spells. Though the rule stipulated that you couldn't attack your opponent until the countdown concluded, there were no rules against getting your defenses in order. Conryu covered himself and Prime in Cloak of Darkness. The countdown reached five and he looked at their team captain. "Which strategy are we using?"

"Attack Plan Three," Caroline said. "You're on defense."

Conryu nodded and mentally prepared to cast his Dispel at the first sign of an incoming attack.

The countdown reached one and everyone raised their hands.

"Zero!"

Everyone started chanting at the same time. The Kingdom team's earth wizard raised a wall of stone and all the Alliance team's spells splashed harmlessly against it.

Crystal chanted a counterspell, and the enemy fortification trembled. For half a second he thought she'd bring it down, but the wall held. Crystal bent over and gasped for breath, totally drained by the attempt.

"She's strong," Crystal said.

Conryu didn't have time to reassure her as spheres of ice, fire, and lightning came arcing in from behind the wall.

Conryu threw up a hand. "Break!"

A dark sphere shot out and negated the fire and lightning spheres, but the ball of ice exploded, showering their team with shards of razor-sharp ice.

Cloak of Darkness protected him from any damage, but Caroline and Leslie weren't so lucky. Both of them collapsed and lay still.

"Dammit!" Conryu said. They'd lost their team captain and their fire wizard—one of their best attackers—in one shot. Worse, with the enemy casting from behind the barricade he couldn't target them with a wide-area Dispel.

More spells came screaming at them. This time he wove a wall of darkness, more out of instinct than because he'd learned that spell. The wall absorbed everything that touched it.

"Crystal, we need cover."

She straightened and chanted. A wall of stone of their own appeared not a moment too soon as a fireball slammed into it.

Conryu shouted for the rest of his teammates, but only Karie, their water wizard, glanced his way. Emily had joined the others on the ground, either unconscious or nearly so. It looked like it was just the three of them.

Karie chanted and spheres of blue energy gathered around her hands. "I'm going for it."

"Wait!" Conryu shouted.

Too late.

She ducked around the wall and a moment later there was a crackle of electricity and a scream.

"Looks like it's just you and me," Conryu said.

"What are we going to do?" Crystal asked.

Conryu clenched his jaw. There was only one way for them to win, but he didn't really want to do it.

"I'm going to have to use some heavy-duty spells. Don't take this the wrong way, but do you mind just staying here out of the way?"

Crystal shook her head. "Do it."

Conryu chanted, "Shroud of all things ending. Cowl of nightmares born. Dark wrap that looks upon all things' doom, Reaper's Cloak!"

The chill shroud settled around him and he pulled the cowl up over his head. Everything changed to shades of black and white.

He stepped out from around the wall of stone, a figure of menace out of your worst nightmare.

The opposing team had emerged from their defensive position. The moment they spotted him three spells shot his way.

They all fizzled when they struck the cloak. He cast, "The chill wind of Hades blow and slay. Death rides in the black-ened air, Reaper's Gale!"

Howling black winds rushed from his hands and engulfed the enemy team. For a moment they were lost from sight.

Conryu focused every speck of willpower he could muster to keep the spell from draining more than the minimal amount of life energy from them.

When the darkness vanished all six opposing wizards lay

on the ground unconscious, their life forces still burning strong in their breasts. The Alliance team had won.

Conryu released his spell. "You can come out now, Crystal."

The wall of stone collapsed and Crystal stepped over the debris. She stared at their unconscious foes and then at him. "Wow."

Conryu grinned. "I'd say this round is ours."

* * *

Lady Tiger stood on an overpass above the street leading to the museum. The bright morning sun warmed her shoulders. She'd gotten little sleep the night before, but adrenaline and determination were working hand in hand to keep her up and focused. Today was it. If she failed there wouldn't be another chance. She would either claim the artifact or die trying. What Lady Dragon would do to her if she failed and survived didn't bear consideration.

The Ministry van had to follow this route if they wanted to reach the front entrance of the museum. In her right hand she grasped a ruby the size of her thumb knuckle. She'd been saving the gem for an emergency, building up the energy stored inside it for years. If ever there was a moment to use it, this was it.

An SUV whizzed past her and a little boy in the back stared at her masked face. It was strange, the little details you noticed in the moments before battle. One time, years ago, on the eve of a battle, she'd spent ten minutes staring at a spider building its web. For some reason it had fascinated her.

The ruby glowed as she poured more fire magic into it. The gem couldn't hold much more and when it detonated, the fireworks should be impressive.

A moment later the Ministry van rounded a bend and came into view. Time to start the dance. "Awaken."

The ruby glowed even brighter and she hurled it at the van. It got brighter and brighter as it grew closer.

The driver tried to swerve, but the gem flew as she willed.

When it struck the grill, the ruby resembled a tiny sun.

An instant later it detonated.

The van flew up, flipped over, and crashed on its roof. The wheels burst into flame and the gas tank exploded, sending a tiny mushroom cloud into the sky.

Drivers honked and swerved around the wreck.

How many cellphones were calling in the attack? Even one was too many.

Lady Tiger leapt off the overpass and flew down, eager to collect her prize before the wizards recovered. It never even crossed her mind that the powerful attack might have killed them all.

She landed beside the burning van and waved her hand. The rear doors ripped off and flew behind her. Inside, battered and bleeding Ministry wizards lay tossed about like crash dummies, groaning and trying to sort themselves out. Two had wounds that appeared fatal.

Lady Tiger grabbed the first container she came to, popped the latches, and looked inside. It held a silvery ring, not what she was after.

She tossed the container aside and grabbed the next one. Another bust.

Container after container went flying until on the third-to-last she found the broken artifact. She stroked the cool metal. At last.

She slipped the semicircle of elf metal into her pocket.

"You there, stop!"

A pair of men in red uniforms drew wooden batons and ran toward her. Stupid men.

She pointed and two streams of flame shot out. The blaze engulfed the men in an instant and reduced them to ash.

The momentary distraction cost her. A powerful force struck her in the chest and sent her flying.

The defensive spell she'd cast earlier absorbed most of the impact as she bounced and then slid across the pavement.

One of the Ministry wizards, her face covered with blood, stumbled out of the wrecked van. She pointed at Lady Tiger and chanted in Angelic.

A single hissed syllable sent a dart of flame streaking in at the bleeding wizard. She dodged, but whatever spell she was attempting failed.

Two more unsteady wizards climbed out of the wreckage.

It was time to make herself scarce. "Father of winds, carry me into your domain. Air Rider."

Lady Tiger shot into the air and raced south. A few seconds later she glanced behind her to find four wizards on her tail and closing.

There was no way she'd have time to open a portal with so many enemies so close behind her.

A lightning bolt streaked past, missing her by a foot.

She countered with a fireball that the pursuing wizards easily avoided. Snarling in annoyance, Lady Tiger wove a random path through the sky as she tried to think how to shake her pursuers.

One on one she could handle any of them, but four on one was more than she had any hope of defeating. She needed help and she knew exactly where to find it.

She twisted in the sky and flew toward the warehouses.

Father Salvador was going to attack early whether he liked it or not.

The thought had barely entered her mind when a wave of dark magic washed over her and sent her tumbling out of the sky.

A hastily cast Gust spell slowed her just enough that nothing broke when her feet hit the cement of the sidewalk. That didn't stop it from hurting like hell.

She cast, "Flames of deepest crimson form a barrier to stop my enemies, Fire Wall!"

And not a moment too soon. A pair of energy blasts struck the wall and got burned away.

While she had a moment's reprieve Lady Tiger studied the area. Unfortunately, she didn't recognize anything. The local shops looked to be in too good a shape to be the slums, but they were also just run down enough not to be in the city center.

The warehouses had to be at least another mile south. How was she going to reach them with four Ministry wizards on her tail? Not through the air, that was certain.

The air! That was it.

She swirled her hands around, altering the wall of fire so it gave off thick, black smoke. Another gesture sent great clouds of it billowing in every direction.

Under the cover of her screen she turned south and ran.

As the smoke continued to spread, the frightened residents came pouring out of their homes and businesses, adding to the chaos. After a moment's hesitation, Lady Tiger slipped off her mask and fell in with the crowd like another frightened civilian.

The trick wouldn't keep them from finding her for long, but hopefully it would buy a minute or two and every second brought her closer to reinforcements. Granted the reinforcements would be just as happy to kill her as the wizards chasing her, but that couldn't be helped.

She managed five blocks before one of her hunters realized the smoke was magical and not caused by something burning. Dark magic washed away her cover.

It was only her imagination, but Lady Tiger would have sworn they were staring at her.

A faint tingle of magic was the only warning she got before light magic chains wrapped her up tight. People ran in every direction when the magic manifested.

She had just space enough to draw a breath. "Dispel."

Dark magic shattered the chains. The Ministry's stated purpose was to protect the people. Time to see if they meant it.

Lady Tiger focused on the largest group of fleeing people. "Flames rage and consume. Fireball!"

A ball of flames twice the size of her head streaked toward the crowd. She ran the opposite way.

When she'd covered two blocks without a spell slamming into her, she slowed and caught her breath. Looked like she'd lost them for now.

Should she keep going toward the warehouses? Her heightened state of awareness saved her as she leapt aside just before a lightning bolt struck where she'd been standing.

Yeah, best keep going toward the warehouses. She hurled a stream of fire toward the source of the attack without aiming.

The neighborhood was becoming familiar. It wouldn't be long now before she reached help.

A chunk of the building beside her exploded, showering her with razor-sharp shards of stone. She winced as several tore into her face and arms.

Finally she stumbled into the yard in front of the warehouses.

No time to waste. She targeted Salvador's building. "Flames rage and consume. Fireball!"

The spell smashed through one of the boarded-up windows and exploded.

A pair of Ministry wizards landed on either side of her. The older of the two, her hair streaked with gray, and sporting a burn mark on her cheek said, "Surrender the artifact and come quietly. There's nowhere left for you to run."

Her head exploded in a shower of gore, spattering Lady Tiger with brains and blood.

Like bees from a kicked hive, soldiers boiled out of two of the warehouses.

The second Ministry wizard threw up a desperate hand and the bullets swerved around her.

Lady Tiger took advantage of the distraction to leap into the air. She needed to find a quiet place to open a portal and escape.

She'd barely gotten into the air when a horrendous, burning pain exploded in her right shoulder. She wobbled in the air and fell, her concentration as broken as her arm.

The cement grew really close really fast.

If she didn't focus she was going to crack her head open.

With a supreme effort of will she slowed her descent so that it only hurt a lot when she hit.

Lady Tiger rolled over on her back and grasped her bloody shoulder. What had hit her?

"Didn't I warn you not to return?" Father Salvador stood over her, a single-shot rifle in his hand. He cracked the breech and a spent cartridge popped out. He dug another round out of his pocket and held it up so she could see it. "Do you recognize this?"

She squinted, but couldn't make anything out. Tears made her vision blurry. Why didn't he shut up and put her out of her misery?

"It's a Death's Head bullet. We got our hands on a whole box of them. It seems someone found them in a storage building of the former Dragon Empire." He slid the cartridge into the breech and closed it. "The church paid a small fortune in gold for that box, but we take great pleasure in the irony of killing wizards with magic weapons."

He cocked the hammer and raised the rifle.

Lady Tiger screamed and breathed flame.

The barrel jerked aside and fired, missing her by inches.

Father Salvador gave a pained shout as his shirt caught on fire. He dropped the gun and rolled around, but her will kept the flames burning.

Lady Tiger got to her feet and limped away. Maybe he'd die of his burns and maybe he wouldn't. Either way, she intended to be long gone before he recovered.

* * *

Father Salvador writhed and screamed as Hell's own fire burned his face and chest. Despite the pain he ground his chest against the dirt, hoping to suffocate the flames. The pain grew until he feared it might drive him mad.

Despite the agony and smell of his own roasting flesh, his mind remained clear. Or perhaps he was becoming delusional in response to the agony he was experiencing. Was this pain what the witches felt when they burned at the stake? Had he done something to displease God that he should be punished so?

Salvador had confessed all his sins before departing on this holy crusade so that couldn't be it. Perhaps God sought to test his resolve by making him suffer under the witch's spell. He was paying the price for allying with a friend of the Devil.

It all became clear to him in that moment. The heathen witch had led them all astray and now he paid for that mistake. Only her death would free him from this pain. Of course, she should have been dead already.

In his mind's eye he saw it clearly. The cursed bullet passing through her skull and splattering her rotted brains on the ground. He'd been only an instant away from inflicting God's justice on the wretched woman, but the moment of his triumph was snatched away by vile magic. Like the demon she truly was, the witch had breathed fire.

Never before had he seen a wizard channel magic, save through her hands. The gout of fire took him totally by surprise. His complete failure led directly to this suffering. He understood that now.

Dear God, if only you take these unholy flames away I swear on my eternal soul to hunt down the blasphemous witch and deliver your divine retribution.

A moment later God answered his prayer and the flames guttered and died. The Almighty had heard his prayer and accepted his devotion. A pact had formed between him and the Almighty. Father Salvador held no doubt that if he failed to slay the witch, his suffering would be eternal.

He forced himself to his knees before strong hands helped lift him to his feet. His eyelids had partially melted and fused together, and a pained howl escaped his lips when he forced them open. Two of his most loyal disciples supported him on either side.

"Father, we must get you to the doctor at once."

"No!" He had no time to waste visiting a doctor. His divine mission would allow for no delays. "Send the order, the attack must begin before the heathens realize we're coming."

Father Salvador jerked his arms free, ignoring the pain and staggering towards the warehouse. "Ready the vans, we must attack immediately."

Rather than leaping to obey, his subordinates looked at each other and then at him. "Are you certain, Father?" the younger asked. "Your flesh is badly blistered and I fear you may get an infection if it isn't tended to at once."

Did the boy dare question God's divine intervention? Salvador was saved from Hell's fire and this fool feared an infection. He drew the pistol at his waist and shot the doubter between the eyes. He collapsed before his weak faith could infect the rest of his divine soldiers.

The surviving acolyte stared at his dead companion. "What have you done?"

"His devotion was weak. We have no room for weaklings in the coming war. How is your faith, Brother Jeremiah?"

"Strong, Father."

"Good. Now send the orders." Salvador holstered his pistol and bent down to retrieve his fallen rifle. "Let the others burn down this city of heathens. We hunt God's true prey."

Father Salvador stalked out, following the trail of blood. The flame of his faith burned hotter than any demon fire. Soon his vision of the witch's death would become reality and God would take his pain for good.

* * *

"The North American Alliance team is the winner!" Jemma said.

The last word still echoed in the stadium when Coach Chort came running in to check on the unconscious members of Conryu's team. On the opposite side of the stadium, the Kingdom coach wasn't far behind.

"Congratulations, Master. You maintained excellent control over the gale. I didn't even sense the Reaper's presence when you donned the cloak."

That had surprised him as well. Usually the Reaper couldn't shut up every time he wore the stupid thing. Maybe he had an important soul to claim and didn't have time to bother Conryu.

"The Reaper can project his awareness to multiple places at once," Prime said. "If he wished to speak to you, it wouldn't matter what else was happening."

"Great." Conryu released the Reaper's Cloak and walked over to join Coach Chort. "Are they okay?"

The truth was, he hadn't gotten very close to his teammates despite the time they'd spent training together. As the only sophomore in the group, they all seemed to regard him as a sort of junior mascot. Not Crystal, but the others. It was weird given his proven abilities, but seniors had been looking down on sophomores since the dawn of school.

"A few bumps and bruises, but nothing that light magic healing won't cure. In fact, if you don't mind lending a hand we can probably get everyone sorted out in a few minutes."

"Sure, but the only healing spell I know is Touch of the Goddess. It might be overkill in this situation."

"Unless you're too tired to cast it, a little overkill won't hurt anything," Coach said. "Caroline got the worst of it. Why don't you start with her?"

Conryu shrugged and knelt beside the team captain. "The gentle light of Heaven washes away all wounds, Touch of the Goddess."

Caroline sat up and rubbed her face. "What hit me?"

Crystal grinned. "I'm pretty sure it was a lightning bolt."

"Ugh! That explains it." She ran a hand through her hair which was currently sticking straight out. "It'll take me forever to tame this back down."

Conryu didn't like to judge, but worrying about her hair after they got their asses handed to them sounded kind of bad. He clamped his mouth shut and moved on to their fire wizard.

"You ought to see what Conryu hit the other guys with." Crystal nodded toward the still-unmoving enemy team across the way.

"You mean we won?" Caroline asked, the disbelief in her voice forcing him to clamp his jaw tighter.

"You bet we did," Crystal said. "Although it would probably be more accurate to say that Conryu won."

Conryu wanted to correct Crystal's assertion that he'd won on his own, but he couldn't do it with a straight face. Unless something wildly unexpected happened tomorrow, he would probably be better off competing without the others. He couldn't, since this was a team event, but facts were facts.

He placed a hand over Leslie's face and cast his healing spell again. Conryu had plenty of energy left and they weren't due to compete again until later this afternoon. A good meal and a nap would wash away any lingering fatigue.

The glow had barely formed when a massive explosion shook the stadium. Crackling energy walls appeared and enclosed the field. Heavy doors crashed down, sealing the tunnels.

Conryu sprang to his feet and looked around. "What's going on?"

Coach Chort shook her head. "I have no idea."

He glanced at Crystal and Caroline, but got only blanks looks in return.

The Kingdom coach left her motionless team and walked over to join them. "It's the emergency security system. We designed it to keep an out-of-control spirit from escaping into the city."

"But we didn't summon any spirits," Conryu said.

"The spell is triggered by any damage to the stadium. We never considered anything else being able to harm the building during a match."

"Since it wasn't a spirit, what did damage the stadium?" Crystal asked.

"Your guess is as good as mine," the Kingdom coach said.

"Kai," Conryu said.

His ninja bodyguard appeared and took a knee. "Chosen?"

Everyone was staring at Kai, but he didn't have time to waste answering their unspoken questions. "See if you can find out what happened."

"Yes, Chosen." Kai vanished and half a second later reappeared. "I can't leave the stadium."

"The protective barrier also seals the area dimensionally," the Kingdom coach said. "It wouldn't do much good to stop a spirit from leaving physically if it could just leave magically."

"Dammit! So how do we escape?" Conryu asked.

"We don't. We're all stuck here until someone on the outside deactivates the ward."

A second explosion rocked the building. They needed information, and the sooner the better.

"Can't we at least look outside?" Conryu asked.

"No, the playing field is completely sealed off from the city. The Ministry made the changes to accommodate the tournament so no magic would escape and potentially harm people passing by."

A third explosion rattled the roof and cracks ran through the cement. It sounded like World War Three outside, and he was stuck in here. Conryu hated it, but for the moment he was stuck.

He only hoped that when someone finally showed up, they didn't have to dig them out from under a pile of rubble.

9

HOTEL RAID

aria finished buttoning her blouse and tied her hair in a ponytail. Not going to the stadium with Conryu this morning sucked, but it was awfully early and she hadn't slept well last night. When she'd mentioned skipping the morning match to Jonny and Kelsie the night before, they suggested surprising him for the afternoon matches. That struck her as an excellent idea so they agreed to meet in her room to watch the morning matches on tv before heading over.

She'd barely stepped out of the bathroom when someone knocked on the door. She opened it and found Jonny and Kelsie waiting.

"Good timing, I just finished getting ready."

"What time does the first match start?" Kelsie asked.

"Eight thirty, but they're on a ten-minute delay so it could very well be over before it even begins." Maria closed the door behind them.

"How do you like their chances?" Jonny asked.

"In a winner-take-all melee, I think they have a good chance," Maria said.

"Cool, I put fifty bucks on Conryu this morning. Got two-to-one odds. The bookie downstairs didn't think much of the Alliance team."

Kelsie smiled and shook her head. "He's never seen Conryu in action. If I had any money, I'd have bet it all on our team."

Jonny grinned. "Yeah, I sort of feel bad for the guy. Not bad enough to refuse his money, but kinda bad."

Maria switched on the tv and put it on the local network. Angus sat between two sportscasters, a man and a woman, behind a long table. The professor looked surprisingly at home. Maybe he'd found his calling.

"The countdown is about to start," the man said. "Let's go to the live feed."

Looked like they planned to pretend that the broadcast was live. Probably gave a sense of immediacy to the audience, especially if they didn't realize it was on a delay.

The screen turned black for half a second and then shifted to show the field. The Alliance team stood facing the Kingdom team. From what she could tell, everyone seemed pretty relaxed.

The countdown began, and the contestants furiously cast defensive spells. Maria recognized most of them, but watching on tv she couldn't get any sense of the power behind the castings.

The countdown hit zero and spells started roaring back and forth. The two teams exchanged blasts and then the Kingdom team raised a wall of stone.

In short order the Alliance team was down to Crystal and Conryu. Kelsie had gnawed her fingernail down to a nub.

Despite her professed confidence, she still worried about him. Maria did too as far as that went.

The Kingdom team came out from behind their defensive structure and advanced. Kelsie gasped when Conryu cast Reaper's Cloak.

He stepped out from behind the wall of stone.

Multiple spells struck him. They all fizzled against his defensive casting. He countered with a black wind that gave Maria chills just seeing it.

The entire Kingdom team fell and Jonny thrust a fist into the air. "Yes, that's a hundred bucks for me. Way to go, bro."

The screen went black again then filled with snow. Maria raised her hand to slap the side of it when the snow cleared. Instead of the sportscasters, the news anchor from the night before appeared. He had a wan, pasty appearance, like he either hadn't slept well or didn't have time to get his makeup done.

Behind him, a scene of burning cars played out. Men in masks sporting machine guns walked through the street shooting at anyone they saw.

For a moment she thought it was from the former Dragon Empire. It seemed every week new fighting broke out over there. The image shifted and Maria recognized the name of a burning department store. She'd walked by it yesterday when she went shopping with her mother.

"Breaking news, it appears terrorists are attacking the city." The anchor licked his sweaty lip and swallowed hard. "The authorities request that everyone remain inside and stay calm. Police and military units are responding and will have things under control soon. When we have new information, we will bring it to you so please stay tuned to this station."

A muffled explosion sounded.

That wasn't on tv.

Maria leapt off the edge of the bed and ran to the window. Smoke was billowing from the ground floor. It looked like a large black van had rammed the doors and caught on fire.

A string of rapid cracks had Kelsie and Jonny on their feet.

"That's machine-gun fire," Jonny said.

Maria took a step toward the door, but he grabbed her arm. "Are you nuts? Don't go out there."

"There might be people in trouble." She tried to pull away, but he held tight.

"There might be people looking to kill us too," he said.

He made an excellent point. Part of her insisted they needed to go help, but another part balked.

The chatter of gunfire grew louder and another smaller explosion went off. "That sounded like a hand grenade," Jonny said. "Whoever these guys are, they aren't screwing around."

Kelsie looked at them with wide eyes. "What are we going to do?"

That was a good question. Maria wished she had a good answer. Unfortunately, despite everything that had happened over the last two years, her combat experience remained limited. Conryu generally handled this sort of thing. She looked to Jonny. He was trained for combat, maybe he knew what they should do.

"Any thoughts?" she asked.

"Yeah, we hunker down and hope they don't kick in the door."

"That's your brilliant suggestion?" Maria couldn't believe what she was hearing. "There might be people that need healing."

"You can't help anyone if you get shot," Jonny said. "Pro-tocol in these situations is you let the cops deal with the threat then the medics go in to help the wounded. Dead healers can't help anyone."

She ground her teeth in frustration, but he had a point. Most of her study so far had focused on healing with a few minor defensive spells thrown in for good measure. She'd only learned two reasonably effective attack spells and wasn't confident with either of them.

Maria glanced at Kelsie. She didn't know what the girl had learned this year, but she didn't get the impression it would be of much use. At least not if Kelsie's reaction to the attack was any indication.

More shouts and gunfire rang out.

Something heavy slammed into their door and the frame splintered. Hiding in their room wasn't an option anymore.

Maria cast, "Sparks fly and bind, Lightning Grasp!"

Her hand crackled with energy and she took a position beside the door. Jonny stood on the opposite side and Kelsie ducked behind one of the chairs.

A second blow smashed the door off its hinges. A man lunged inside, a rifle to his shoulder.

Maria put a hand on his back and released her spell. Lightning crackled into him and he collapsed. A second man followed.

The soldier was so distracted by what happened to his friend that he didn't notice when Jonny came up behind him, wrapped an arm around his neck, and squeezed.

The man flailed and fought. His gun fired several times into the ceiling. Finally, he collapsed and Jonny let him slide to the floor.

He picked up the rifle, checked how many bullets were left in the clip, and slammed it into place.

"Well," Jonny said as he bent down to collect the ammo belt

on the man he choked out. "We can't hide if there's no door. Shall we step out and see what kind of trouble we can get into?"

Maria bent down and applied Lightning Grasp to the unconscious man. The spell lasted an hour—win or lose, the fight should be finished before the effect ran out.

"That's what I wanted to do in the first place," she said.

Kelsie peeked out from behind the chair. "I'm coming."

"Do you know any offensive spells?" Maria asked.

"Just a couple weak ones." She bit her lip. "I wish Conryu was here."

"So do I," Maria said. "But he's not, and we can't always depend on him to be. We just have to do our best and hope we can make a difference."

Kelsie straightened and nodded. She looked determined if nothing else.

Jonny rushed to the smashed-in door frame and peeked out. "The hall's clear. Let's move."

"Wait." Maria put a hand on his back and murmured Lightning Shield. "It's not much, but it's the strongest defensive spell I know."

"I'll take whatever I can get, thanks."

Jonny stepped out into the hall and raised his rifle, Maria followed, and Kelsie brought up the rear. The next door down the hall had been kicked in.

Johnny peeked inside and immediately slammed the door. "You don't want to look in there."

He hurried down the hall, but Maria paused just outside the door. She knew what she'd find inside, but if someone was wounded and playing dead... Better to be certain.

Inside the room, three bodies lay on the floor riddled with bullets. Blood covered everything. Her breath caught in her throat. Her stomach churned. It was only through sheer force of will she kept from throwing up.

She could do nothing for them. No one could.

Turning away from the horrible sight she rejoined the others outside. Jonny angled across the hall to the elevator control panel and pressed the button.

"It's dead, probably an emergency response."

"So what are we going to do?" Kelsie asked.

"Take the stairs, I guess," Jonny said.

"The stairwell is at the end of the hall on your right," Maria said.

He brought his rifle up once more to the ready position and led the way. They passed more smashed-in doors, but Maria didn't feel the need to check inside.

When they reached the end of the hall, he looked at them and held up a hand. Maria might not have had any military training, but she recognized the sign for "wait a minute."

Jonny ducked around the corner and immediately retreated ahead of a spray of bullets. "Back! Back!"

The three of them ran up the hall towards their room. Maria looked over her shoulder and saw six men round the corner. Five of them had machine guns and one, she was fairly sure, carried a rocket launcher.

Kelsie paused and chanted. Gray mist filled the hall, obscuring their view.

They hugged the wall as bullets zipped down the passage.

Only a few steps.

Maria panted as she ran.

They slipped into her room. There was no door to lock and she had no way to seal the entrance.

Jonny stood in the doorway and fired down the hall. His weapon nearly deafened her.

An explosion outside the door sent them all flying.

Maria struggled to her knees in time to see the soldiers rushing into the room, their rifles raised.

* * *

Heather paced back and forth in front of the window in her room. She'd begged off going to the morning matches, claiming to not be feeling well. It was true enough, especially after her last conversation with Malice. The evil old woman had insisted that Heather kill Conryu's current girl-friend so that he might turn to one of her choosing in his time of grief. She didn't know whether to be terrified or disgusted at the emotionless tone Malice used to give the order, maybe a little of both.

While Heather hated losing to anyone, killing the competition pushed the envelope beyond where even she was willing to go. Willing or not, Malice made it clear that if she didn't follow orders she'd lose everything.

Could she kill someone? It wouldn't be that difficult, the girl was just a sophomore. She hadn't reached her full magical potential and wouldn't for another year. Any number of spells would do the job quickly and efficiently. The problem was, Heather had never killed anyone. She didn't know if she had the stomach for it. That sort of squeamishness might surprise some of her detractors who thought she had a heart of ice.

She paused in her pacing and glanced at herself in the mirror. Dark smudges ringed her bloodshot eyes. She hadn't gotten more than a few hours' sleep last night. Damn Malice and her precious mission.

It had seemed like an easy job. Make some quick bucks, no big deal. She'd slept with plenty of men to advance her career.

It wasn't a problem and the way she spent money, Heather always needed more. It wasn't easy maintaining a supermodel's lifestyle even on a supermodel's income. Now look at her.

An explosion rocked the building, startling her out of her thoughts. What the hell was that? She threw open the curtains and looked out.

Nothing on this side of the building. She held her breath and listened. A string of rapid cracks filled the air. Was that gunfire?

She flipped on the tv and switched it to the news. The reporter was blathering about terrorists in the streets. She turned it off again seconds later. This may be the opportunity she needed. She might not have to kill anyone after all.

Heather pulled on her aqua robe and stepped out into the hall. Nothing happening on this floor.

She made the short walk to the elevator and pressed the call button.

Nothing.

The stairs then.

It was weird, walking down the empty hall, her steps echoing around her. Everyone left for the stadium an hour ago, so she had the whole floor to herself. Oh well, a few idiots with guns was nothing a skilled wizard couldn't handle.

As she got closer to the stairwell door, she cast a simple defensive spell that would turn aside any bullets that came her way. She pulled open the door and found herself face-to-face with a pair of men wearing black uniforms and carrying machine guns. They stared at her and she stared right back at them. For a moment no one did anything.

Heather came to her senses first and cast a quick offensive spell. A spray of water drenched the two men and froze them solid. They collapsed on the landing and she stepped over them. The ice prison would hold them for several hours. It wouldn't cause any major damage, though they'd both probably end up with terrible frostbite.

She ran down the steps to the next floor two at a time. When she reached the landing, she peeked out the door. Conryu's friends were all running her way down a fog-filled hall. Bullets whizzed through the mist. Heather flinched when one buried itself in the wall a little to her left. She closed the door and resumed her observations through the window.

The students lunged into an open doorway. Soldiers emerged from the fog moments later. One of them carried a shoulder rocket launcher. He aimed it at the empty doorway and squeezed the trigger.

A huge fireball burst to life. It looked like she would get her wish.

* * *

Maria coughed and choked on smoke. The room was a blur. She rubbed her eyes, trying to clear her sight. Beside her Jonny groaned and rolled over on his side.

Shouts and movement drew her gaze. Dark blobs ran in through the shattered door. She blinked again, but still couldn't make out any details.

A glint of light caught her attention and drew her gaze to the barrel of a gun. It was pointed at her head. Suddenly everything came into focus.

She was about to die, helpless and kneeling on the floor. She hadn't imagined it ending like this. Not that she'd imagined it ending any other way.

A blinding flash forced her to close her eyes. For a moment

she feared the soldier had fired, but when no burning pain struck her, she realized something else had happened.

That's when the screams started.

Maria opened her eyes a fraction, just enough to see the soldiers writhing in the sea of flames. She closed her eyes tight again. Men burning to death wasn't something she had any desire to watch. Not even when the men wanted her dead. It also wasn't something she had any desire to experience. Hopefully, whoever had set them on fire was on her side.

A second later, everything fell silent. She risked opening her eyes again. Of the men in black no sign remained save for the scorch marks on the ceiling. A small figure with blond hair sticking out every which way stood in the open doorway. She wore red pajamas. How did someone's daughter end up on her floor?

This was no place for a kid. She scrambled to her feet and took a step toward her.

"What's going on out here?" When she spoke Maria recognized Conryu's friend Sonja. "I'm trying to rest."

"I'm sorry we bothered you," Maria said. "But thank you for saving our lives."

Sonja peered around as if trying to figure out what was going on. "I thought someone had the tv turned up really loud, then I opened my door and saw all these soldiers everywhere."

"It looks like the city's been invaded." Maria glanced up and down the hall, but found no more men in black.

"Invaded? Invaded by who?" Sonja asked.

"I don't know," Maria said. "From what happened here and what I saw on the news it looks like they're serious, whoever they are."

"They are." Maria turned to see Heather walking down the

hall. "I met two of them on the stairs down here. They were dressed in the uniform of the Blessed Army."

"Blessed Army?" Sonja asked.

"Religious fanatics who like nothing better than killing wizards," Maria said. "How did so many of them enter the city?"

Jonny and Kelsie had gotten their wits about them and joined Maria by the door.

"We studied the Blessed Army in strategy class," Jonny said. "Our commanders said they were the enemy we were most likely to have to actually fight."

"Did they have any suggestions about the best way to do so?" Kelsie asked.

Jonny shook his head. "Nothing that would apply to this situation. This is pure urban warfare. There could be an enemy around every corner. I still say our best bet is to hole up somewhere and wait for the authorities to come and deal with these guys. Worst case scenario, we might get shot by our own people."

Sonja groaned. "I'm all for going back to bed, but I'm afraid I won't be able to rest now. In fact, I'm in a mood to show these assholes what happens when you wake up a sick wizard."

"We have a responsibility to protect the civilians," Heather said.

Maria glared at her. "What are you doing here anyway? Shouldn't you be at the stadium with the team?"

Heather brushed her hair out of her face. "I felt like I was coming down with something this morning too. Coach Chort agreed that I should rest and join them for the afternoon matches."

"I suspect there aren't going to be any afternoon matches," Maria said.

"At the very least," Sonja said, "we should check on Crystal's parents and the rest of the guests on this floor. Maybe we can seal off the stairwells and keep any more soldiers from entering."

Maria nodded. It was a good compromise. "Okay. Does anyone have any objections?"

Kelsie and Jonny both shook their heads.

"I can create walls of ice to seal off the stairwells," Heather said. "That should hold off anyone trying to come up for a little while."

Jonny found an undamaged gun and took the lead. They went door to door, finding more corpses than survivors. Every survivor they found Maria directed toward Sonja's room. It was near the center of the floor and she was certain no bodies littered the floor. A small spot of luck, Crystal's family was still safe, unlike many other, less fortunate people.

After clearing all the rooms and finding no more soldiers, they headed to the nearest stairwell. Heather chanted and conjured her wall of ice while everyone else kept watch.

"It's a slaughter," Jonny said. "You study war and combat in school, but seeing it in real life is something else. I thought I'd be able to handle it, but my hands are shaking."

Maria squeezed his shoulder. It was taking everything she had just to keep it together, but if he lost it, it might start a chain reaction. "You're doing great. This is a new situation for all of us."

"Thanks." Jonny offered her a weak smile.

Heather finished the wall of ice and wiped sweat from her brow. "That's one down, three to go."

"Can you manage three more?" Maria asked.

"Oh, don't worry about me. This is nothing for a fully trained wizard."

Maria's face twisted. "I'm thrilled to hear it."

Arrogant bitch. She wanted to punch Heather's perfect face in, but this wasn't the time or the place. The time would come though, she knew it.

* * *

L ady Tiger limped through the slums and away from the warehouse. Her spell had ended moments ago. If he survived, Father Salvador wouldn't be long getting on her trail. Hopefully, the spell killed him, but in her heart of hearts she knew it hadn't. His mad devotion would give him all the strength he needed. That same madness would also compel him to hunt her down and finish what he started.

She groaned and leaned against a building. Though there was little time to spare, she needed to rest, just for a moment. She closed her eyes and listened. Other than her ragged breathing, only silence filled the air. The locals had abandoned the area. Good decision on their part. It never ceased to amaze her, how rats, both human and animal, recognized when the time to escape had arrived.

Overhead, the sky was clear. Under ordinary circumstances it would've been a simple matter for her to race into the sky and fly to safety. Today, just thinking about casting a flight spell made her head throb. Speaking of throbbing, her shoulder sent jagged blasts of pain into her with each heart-beat. She glanced back the way she'd come and found a trickle of blood. Her hunters would have no difficulty tracking her with a trail like that to follow.

A quick glance around the area revealed little she could use. The buildings were all in various states of decay, but there was one in a little better shape than the rest. The sign over the door said "Boardinghouse." She might find something there to use for a bandage.

She staggered across the street, up the steps, and through the door. No one stood behind the counter so she just reached over and grabbed a room key. She made her way down a short hall to room three and unlocked it.

Yellow-stained sheets covered a narrow bed. It didn't look like anyone had changed them in months. Well, desperate times led to desperate actions. She sat on the edge of the mattress and tore her robe open. Her stomach twisted at the pain but she kept going. When the wound had been exposed, she focused her will and summoned fire into her hand. It was very difficult for wizards to heal themselves, but she could still stop the bleeding.

Clenching her jaw against the pain, she pressed the fire into the injury.

Everything went black.

* * *

Maria darted a glance at Heather as the group marched down to the final stairwell. Aside from her face having gone a bit pale, the woman appeared to be handling the casting of so many powerful spells without difficulty. Little as Maria may have thought of her as a person, she couldn't deny Heather's skill as a wizard. Under other circumstances, she would've happily hung Heather out one of the windows by her ankles, but right now having an experienced wizard to back them up came as a huge relief.

Jonny ran up to the stairwell door, kicked it open, and checked the landing. "Clear!"

He'd done it four times now and each time he seemed to

gain a little more confidence. Jonny stepped away from the doorway, grinned at Heather, and said, "You're up."

Heather raised her hands and began the familiar cadence of the wall of ice spell. Even though she didn't understand the words, Maria could almost recite the spell along with her. The ambient moisture in the air had barely begun to gather when Maria heard the tread of heavy boots coming up the steps.

"We've got incoming." Jonny raised his rifle and aimed it into the stairwell.

Sonja moved to join him, fire dancing around her hands. The mist gathered more slowly and Maria knew why.

"You need to move away, Sonja. Your fire magic is interfering with Heather's spell."

"Who's going to hold back the soldiers?" Sonja asked.

"I got this," Johnny said.

Sonja let the fire vanish and stepped aside. A moment later the first black-clad soldier appeared at the foot of the stairs.

Jonny opened fire, driving the first man back. The mists continued to grow thicker and ice formed on the floor.

The Blessed Army soldiers returned fire. Bullets pinged all around the doorway. Jonny fired a few more shots as the ice continued to thicken.

He staggered and fell on his butt. The ice reached three-quarters of the way up the doorway. Bullets hammered into it, but failed to penetrate.

Maria rushed over and knelt beside Jonny. She found no blood on his chest and when she felt around none of the bones appeared broken. Her spell had held.

"Are you okay?"

"Yeah, I think so. That hurt like a son of a bitch."

Heather lowered her hands and sighed. "There, that'll hold for a little while."

"Good. We need to get somewhere safe so I can heal this bruise on Jonny's chest." Maria helped him up and Kelsie hurried over to grab his gun. Maria doubted she had any idea how to shoot it, but they might need it later.

Sonja led the way to the nearest room and pushed the door open. It was one they'd evacuated earlier, so no bodies covered the floor. And thank goodness for that, Maria couldn't have dealt with cleaning up a slaughterhouse.

Once they were inside and the door closed Sonja collapsed on the bed. "I need to rest." So saying she closed her eyes and was snoring in moments.

Maria guided Johnny to one of the chairs and sat him down. "I'll have you fixed up in no time, just hold still."

He grinned. "Seems like you spend a lot of time fixing me up."

"Well, next time don't get shot. Now be quiet so I can concentrate."

She started casting while across the room Kelsie relaxed in the second chair and put her feet up. Light magic gathered and surrounded Johnny's injury. The damage wasn't bad enough to require a full healing field. It was nowhere near as serious as what happened when Lady Raven struck him.

Everyone could rest for an hour while she finished her spell. Once they'd caught their breath, they'd have some serious decisions to make.

* * *

The soft murmur of voices brought Lady Tiger back to her senses. With awareness came pain, her shoulder screamed at her and she let slip a soft whimper. She clamped her hand across her mouth to seal off any more noises.

Whoever she heard had to be either after her or up to no good. Whatever the case, she was in no shape to fight off a child, much less an adult with a gun.

"We have to be getting close," a male voice said. He sounded vaguely familiar but her thoughts were too jumbled to place him.

"Oh we are, I can smell her corrupt soul," Father Salvador said.

So he'd come after her. It wasn't that she doubted he would, more that she'd allowed herself an instant of hope that he might not have survived the blast. Lady Tiger should have realized by now that hoping was a waste of effort.

She turned her awareness inward and tried to summon her magic. A backlash headache set the room spinning. She'd be getting no magical help. Even at perfect health she wouldn't have been able to physically fight off Father Salvador and whoever he brought with him. Much as it galled her, she needed to find a place to hide.

This room was no good, the trail of blood she left came right to it. But with Father Salvador out in the hall there was no escape that way. Lady Tiger racked her brain and looked around. There had to be something.

The only other piece of furniture in the dumpy room was a rickety wardrobe. If she hid there Father Salvador would find her in a second.

Lady Tiger slid off the bed and tiptoed to the tiny bathroom. Her eyes widened. Someone had smashed a hole through the bathroom wall into the next apartment. Why someone would do that she had no idea nor did she care. It was the perfect escape route.

As quietly as possible in her injured state, she eased her way through the opening, careful not to rub her wounded shoulder against one of the studs. The next apartment wasn't in any better shape than this one. The priest would find her on the other side of the hole the moment he arrived.

Only one option remained. When they entered the apartment next door, she would slip out into the hall and escape. As plans went this didn't please her, but she had no other choice. At least she'd stopped bleeding all over the place. She just needed a little distance between her and them and maybe she could hide.

Lady Tiger held her breath and listened. "She's gotta be in here," the first voice said.

She grimaced. It sounded like only two of them were after her, but if she guessed wrong and a third man remained out in the hall, she died.

A loud crash sounded when someone kicked down the door. "Come out, come out, wherever you are," Father Salvador said.

Ignoring the taunt, she kept listening for footsteps in the hall. It didn't sound like anyone was out there. She needed to move before they found the hole in the bathroom wall.

She steeled herself and stepped out of the room. A strangled gasp of relief slipped out when she found it empty. With a final glance back the way she'd come, Lady Tiger tiptoed down the hall. At the end of the passage she came to a door and eased it open.

She nearly wept when she found just another apartment. There should've been an emergency exit or something here. Not that she imagined the owners of this dump were concerned with safety. Her options exhausted, Lady Tiger entered the apartment and eased the door shut as quietly as she could.

In five minutes at most Father Salvador would find his way

down to this room. This unit was in a little bit better shape than the others, but that wasn't saying much. A bed with reasonably clean sheets filled the bulk of the space along with a side table and wardrobe. Nothing that would do for a hiding place. A single door led to a tiny bathroom with a window.

Like a lost explorer in the desert offered a glass of water, her eyes locked on that window. It had a latch, which meant it opened. It was a narrow opening, but if she forced herself, she should be able to wriggle through. But oh God was it going to hurt.

Pain was better than death which was better than failure. Lady Tiger climbed up on the toilet and flicked open the window. It opened out into a trash-strewn alley. The drop only measured about eight feet. Even injured she should be able to handle that.

Distant, muffled voices reached her. No more time for debate.

Using her good arm she grabbed the frame and pulled herself up. Her head fit through okay then it was time to get her injured shoulder through. She clenched her jaw and lunged.

Her sight went gray for a moment, but she was halfway out. Wriggling and pushing with her good arm and legs she made it the rest of the way through and dropped to the pavement. The impact sent lightning bolts lancing into her shoulder, but she refused to pass out again.

Focusing through the pain she limped away from the apartment building. She needed to find somewhere to rest so she could open a portal out of this miserable city.

* * *

Heather tried to still her trembling hands as she watched Maria cast her healing spell. The girl had skill and when her power reached its full potential, she would make a fine wizard. If she lived that long.

Though Heather liked to claim she stayed in practice, she'd used more magic today than she had since her last tournament. Not that lack of practice should have affected her power, you were what you were until you died. In the back of her skull the first faint throbs of a backlash headache built. If there'd been one more stairwell, she doubted she would've had the strength to seal it. Not that she would have admitted such a thing.

She surveyed the room, trying not to be obvious about it. The little fire wizard snored away on the bed. Malice's granddaughter sat with her feet up and appeared dead to the world. Finally, Maria stood beside the injured boy and both of them faced away from her.

There'd never be a better opportunity. How she'd escape after killing the girl was another question. At the moment it didn't look like there were many people in a position to stop her from simply walking away. Weak as she was, Heather had power enough to deal with a half-dead fire wizard, a weakling girl, and an ordinary boy. She'd have to be careful with Kelsie, since she feared what Malice might do if she accidentally killed the girl.

What it came down to, was whether she valued her career more than someone's life. Thinking back to the way Maria looked at her, like Heather was little better than a common whore, she decided that Maria's life wasn't worth as much as her career.

Chanting a spell would surely draw attention better avoided, so Heather gathered magic using nothing but willpower. It took longer and set her head to pounding, but soon an ice dagger began to form in her hand. As it continued to expand and harden she hid the weapon behind her back.

Just when she feared her head might explode from the backlash, the spell ended. Ice as hard as steel filled her fist. She squeezed so tight her knuckles ached.

Now or never.

She raised her blade to strike.

"Break!"

The ice dagger shattered. She stared at Kelsie. Of all the people she'd imagined getting in her way, Malice's weakling granddaughter didn't even rate a spot on the list.

Her moment of shock cost her. Maria chanted, "Sparks fly and bind, Lightning Grasp!"

Before Heather could react the spell coursed through her body. Her muscles spasmed and she collapsed to the floor.

Maria stood over her and stared down. "I knew it was a mistake to trust you."

Her foot crashed into the side of Heather's head and everything went dark.

* * *

Father Salvador snarled when he found the hole in the bathroom wall. The sneaky witch had found a way past them, God curse her. It shouldn't have surprised him, like any vermin she knew how to hide.

He staggered a step and leaned against the wall, panting for breath.

"Are you alright, Father?" Jeremiah asked.

The pain in his face and chest was nearly unbearable, but

bear it he would. The witch's betrayal would not go unavenged.

"I'm fine. We need to get after her before she gets any further away."

He ignored Jeremiah's concerned frown and kicked the door out of his way. He turned left and marched down the hall. It was the only way for her to go. They'd have heard her if she tried to walk past them.

Room after room revealed nothing but the filth the locals lived in. At last he came to the final door on the floor. She had to be in there. He kicked the door in and raised his rifle. Nothing but another empty room.

"Why do you taunt me, Lord?" he shouted at the ceiling.

With the butt of his rifle Father Salvador smashed the wardrobe to pieces. Of course the witch wasn't inside. He looked under the bed, but again came up empty. That left the small bathroom. Could she possibly escape him twice the same way?

He slammed the bathroom door open and his gaze darted to the open window. He bared his teeth and climbed up on the toilet. A flash of red across the street caught his eye.

There she was!

He thrust the barrel of his rifle out the window and drew a bead. His finger touched the trigger just as she moved out of sight behind another building.

Damn her! He was so close.

"She's escaping!" he shouted. "Hurry, before she gets away."

The two of them raced to the entrance, went outside, and ran around the apartment building. Father Salvador looked back and spotted the window through which she'd escaped. He studied the ground, but found no more blood. He couldn't lose her, not now. Not when he was so close.

"Father, look." Jeremiah bent down and pointed at some scuff marks in the dirt.

It wasn't much, but they had nothing else to go on. They moved out, carefully following the marks.

He would find her. No matter what it took or how long he had to spend. He would find her.

10

TRAPPED

C onryu paced back and forth like a caged lion. Every few seconds he glanced up at the roof, frowned, and resumed his path. Prime watched his every move, but the scholomantic wisely kept silent. Conryu was in no mood for conversation. He wanted out of the stadium, needed out. God only knew what was happening out there, but the constant explosions sounded like a war. Maria and the others might be in trouble and he was stuck here. It took all his self-control not to scream.

Another muffled blast sounded, the fifth in the last two minutes. Coach Chort had the rest of the team awake and on their feet. They didn't look entirely steady, but at least they were conscious. The Kingdom coach also had most of her girls sitting up and staring blearily around. Conryu was relieved his spell hadn't done too much damage. In hindsight maybe using Reaper's Gale was a little excessive for a sporting event. Of course, they'd won, so who was he to say.

"Sit down, Conryu," Coach said. "You're making me nervous."

"Sorry," Conryu said. "I can't rest, not knowing what's happening."

"None of us like it, but there's nothing we can do."

"Has anyone tried dispelling the ward?" he asked.

"Our best wizards created it to withstand anything that might be unleashed during the tournament," the Kingdom coach said.

Conryu glanced at Prime. "What do you think, pal?"

"I think if you're determined to leave, Master, there's no wizard powerful enough to hold you."

Conryu grinned. "You read my mind again. What do you say we try a Death Spiral?"

"That should certainly do it," Prime said.

"Whoa, whoa." The Kingdom coach hurried over waving her hands. "If your Death Spiral successfully breaches the wards you'll blow a hole in the roof."

"That was sort of my plan," Conryu said. "We can just say whoever's attacking the city did it."

The Kingdom coach stared at him for a moment. "You're serious."

He nodded. "You don't have to use that excuse, but I intend to get out of here if I can."

She chewed her lip and rubbed the bridge of her nose. "You can try, but I don't hold out much hope. I was here when they wove those wards, they are the strongest I've ever seen."

"Thanks for the warning." Conryu started towards the far end of the field. If any debris came falling down, he didn't want to hit anyone. "Assuming I'm successful, you might want to send out anyone who can fight as soon as they are able. From the sounds of it, the defenders of the city are going to need all the help they can get."

A good fifty yards away from the others, Conryu raised his right hand and chanted. "Deepest darkness twist and writhe. Grind and smash what I despise. Break through bonds and destroy all barriers, Death Spiral."

When he'd gone through the spell three times and built up all the power he could he gave a final twirl of his finger and released the gathered energy. The dark magic struck the ward which sparked to life as the two magics battled.

The battle wasn't lengthy. In less than a minute his spiral drilled through and slammed into the roof sending girders and concrete flying outward. Hopefully there was no one nearby for the rubble to land on. Or maybe he should hope some of the enemy was nearby.

"Kai, you should be able to reach Maria now. Hurry and make sure she's okay."

Kai didn't waste any breath appearing to confirm his order. In fact, by now she should be at the hotel. He needed to hurry and join her as soon as possible.

"Father of winds, carry me into your domain. Air Rider."

He leapt and flew out the hole he'd smashed in the roof. Outside the city was on fire. Dozens of buildings belched smoke from holes blown in the side of them. More cars than he cared to count were reduced to blackened shells. The sound of machine-gun fire echoed from every direction and the explosions that sounded muffled inside now seemed far louder.

As he gained altitude and looked around, Conryu spotted a pair of dragon manes battling a cloud of wizards. It reminded him of a crow being harassed by a flock of sparrows. Although in this case the crow could breathe fire.

That wasn't his fight. Conryu turned toward the hotel and willed himself to maximum speed. It shouldn't take him thirty seconds to join Kai. He said a silent prayer that Maria would be okay until he arrived.

* * *

M aria ran over and hugged Kelsie. "You saved me, thank you."

Kelsie beamed. "I finally got the spell to work."

Maria choked a little. She'd only now gotten Dispel to work? If Kelsie's spell had failed Maria might've gotten her throat cut. Her whole body trembled as she realized how close to death she'd come.

"Conryu will be so proud of me when I tell him. He's been helping me work on it off and on for months now."

"I'm certainly glad you got it working when you did," Maria said.

Jonny scrambled to his feet. "My question is, what are we going to do with our two heavy hitters out of action?"

That was a good question. Hopefully, the walls of ice would hold and they wouldn't need to figure out what they were going to do. If the walls failed, well, they'd just have to do their best. The three of them were all that stood between three dozen unarmed and inexperienced civilians and who knew how many soldiers that wanted them all dead.

"I'm open to suggestions," Maria said.

"I don't know," Jonny said. "Don't you guys have any spells that can stop them?"

"I can use the mist spell again," Kelsie said. "But all it does is make it hard for them to see."

"That might buy us a minute or two and provide cover if we need to run for it," Jonny said. "Every little bit helps."

They both looked at Maria. "Lightning Grasp is my best offensive spell, but it only works if I can contact the target. I have next to nothing for ranged magic."

"Well, I've got three clips plus what's in the gun now so about a hundred rounds. If it comes to a firefight that won't last two minutes." He shook his head. "I think it's fair to say we're pretty well screwed."

"That's putting it mildly," Maria said.

As if to add an exclamation point to her statement, an especially loud explosion shook the floor. There was only one thing they could be blowing up and that was one of the ice walls. With Heather unconscious, they'd become weaker than normal. She'd known it was going to happen, but the alternative was leaving somebody that wanted to kill her awake and active. It was a crappy choice, but she'd made the only one she could.

"Can anyone tell where that came from?" she asked.

"Sounded like the east corner," Jonny said. He pointed to his left. "If they're coming, it will be from that way."

"What if we shove the table out into the hall to make a barricade," Kelsie said.

Jonny nodded. "That's not a bad idea. It won't hold for long, but it might buy us a minute or two."

Right now, every minute was precious. The three of them worked together to shove the table out into the hall. It looked pathetic to Maria, but it was all they could do.

Sonja never so much as flinched while they worked. She'd read about wizards who were ill using magic. Even simple spells drained them faster than normal. Maria seriously doubted the little fire wizard would wake up for hours.

Maria looked down at Heather and grimaced. It would be so easy to leave her behind.

She sighed. No, however horrible she might be, Maria couldn't leave her to die.

Jonny crouched behind the table. Footsteps were getting closer every moment.

"You want me to fill the hall with mist?" Kelsie asked.

"Not yet," Johnny said. "I'll signal you when I'm ready."

Maria placed her hand on Kelsie's back and cast Lightning Shield. It'd saved Jonny though the bullet left a nasty bruise. It might be the difference between life and death.

"Thanks," Kelsie said when she finished. "What are we going to do about the other two?"

"I know a spell that will let us move them, but I'll need you to help me position them before I cast it."

The two girls struggled to move the unconscious women side by side. When they finally finished both of them were gasping and drenched in sweat.

Outside, Jonny started shooting. Sounded like the guests had arrived.

She nodded Kelsie into place by the door and began her spell. A few seconds later a glowing disk appeared under Heather and Sonya. It lifted them both up off the ground and hovered there. Energy rushed out of Maria. She wouldn't be able to maintain the spell for long.

The volume of gunfire picked up and Jonny shouted, "Now!"

Kelsie cast her mist spell.

"Let's move," Jonny said.

Maria ran out the door, the golden disk floating along behind her.

They rushed through the halls towards the central room

where they'd left the civilians. If a last stand was to be made, it would have to be outside that room. If they failed here, everyone would die.

"They're coming," Jonny said. "Take cover in the doorway."

Maria stepped inside and hid on the left side of the opening while Jonny crouched opposite her. He lined up his rifle and waited.

"What's going on?" a woman at the rear of the room asked.

Maria held a finger to her lips. "They're coming."

Jonny fired a pair of shots and a hail of return fire forced him to duck back out of danger.

The muscle at the corner of his jaw bunched and he lunged out to shoot again. From her position, Maria couldn't see what was happening. She felt useless, hiding where it was safe and letting Jonny take all the risks.

A bullet slammed into him and sent Jonny sprawling. He groaned and struggled to get up.

One of the soldiers appeared in the doorway and Maria cast, "Sparks fly and bind, Lightning Grasp!"

She grabbed his leg and he fell twitching to the floor.

Maria scrambled aside as another soldier took his place. The barrel of his gun looked awfully big when he pointed it at her.

She had no time to cast another spell.

His finger closed on the trigger.

Maybe her protective spell would stop the first couple shots, but after that...

A black sword pierced his chest sending the barrel flying toward the ceiling where it stitched a line in the drywall.

Kai spun him around and shoved him toward his approaching companions.

The ninja moved like a shadow amongst the men, appearing and vanishing into the borderland.

Every time she appeared the black sword lashed out, taking an arm or a leg from an unfortunate soldier.

Panicked fire filled the hall and riddled the walls with bullets. In seconds only silence filled the hall. Kai appeared in the doorway and bowed. "Are you unharmed?"

She nodded. "Conryu?"

"The Chosen is well and on his way. He requested that I travel ahead in case you required aid. It seems he was wise to send me."

"Yeah, I'd say so," Maria agreed. "Can you keep watch? I need to check on Jonny."

Kai bowed again and vanished. Maria didn't worry about the woman abandoning them. From what Maria had seen, she seemed wholly devoted to Conryu. If he sent her to protect them, she'd die before she failed him.

Jonny groaned and she knelt beside him. "Are you okay?"

"I'm alive. You need to work on that spell, get it to stop the bullet from hitting so hard."

"Better a bruise than a hole in your chest. Hold still and I'll take care of it."

Kelsie joined them and asked, "Who was that girl?"

"A friend of Conryu's. It's a long story, but rest assured she's on our side."

And thank goodness for that. If Kai hadn't showed up when she did, Maria didn't like to think about what would have happened.

* * *

The hotel entrance billowed smoke and a group of soldiers in security uniforms exchanged fire with another group in black that was mixed with young people wearing ripped jeans and t-shirts. It looked like a standoff. Both sides hunkered down behind vehicles that resembled Swiss cheese. He couldn't deal with that now.

He swung around to the back side of the building and flew even with the top floor. Conryu pointed at the thick glass. "Shatter!"

A hole big enough for him to fly through disintegrated. He landed in the hall not far from his room. "Do you sense anything, Prime?"

"Four people are approaching from directly ahead, and there's a large group on the floor below."

The big group had to be the guests. Maria would be down there tending to the injured. She'd be fine. Kai would protect her.

"Master, they're getting closer," Prime said.

Conryu released his flight spell and cast, "Spirits of earth, strong and firm. A barrier form to prove your worth. Diamond Skin!"

A moment later four punks in leather jackets rounded the corner in front of him. The four of them stared at Conryu a moment before opening up with their machine guns.

The bullets pinged off him with no more effect than flies on a windshield.

Conryu raised a hand. "Gust!"

A two-hundred-mile-an-hour burst of straight-line wind shot from his hand and slammed into them. The spell swept the madmen up and slammed them into the wall with enough force to leave impressions in the drywall. They slid down and didn't move.

As he walked past Conryu disintegrated their weapons. He'd thoroughly explored the floor when he first arrived so it took only a few minutes to locate stairs down.

He took them two at a time and at the bottom found a wall of ice slowly melting and blocking his way. Looked like Heather had done her part. Nothing like an army to get you to do something useful.

Conryu gestured and the wall vanished in a burst of dark magic. He stepped into an empty hall.

"Which way?"

"Left, Master. You're getting good at wielding dark magic without a spell. Though I probably shouldn't encourage you."

"Thanks." Ten steps later Kai appeared beside him. "Is she okay?"

"Yes, Chosen, though it was a near thing. All of your friends survived. Some of the other guests didn't."

Conryu grimaced and nodded. Kai vanished into Hell and he continued on his way. It was a shame about the others, but he couldn't do anything about it. Maria wasn't hurt and he hated to admit it, but that mattered more than anything else to him.

He rounded a bend and found a hall full of bodies with severed limbs. Kai hadn't held back today and he didn't blame her. Anyone that went into a hotel to kill innocent people deserved what they got.

"Maria!"

A moment later she emerged from a room just down the hall. Conryu had never seen a more beautiful sight in all his life. His heart raced and he ran toward her.

They met in the middle of the carnage. She leapt into his

arms and he swung her around before kissing her. He held her until Jonny said, "Get a room, dude."

He let Maria go after a final kiss and grinned. "Shouldn't be hard, we're in a hotel after all."

Conryu bumped fists with Jonny. "Good to see you, bro."

"Likewise. I'd have been here sooner, but there was some trouble at the stadium. Kai made it in time to help I see." Conryu and Maria joined Jonny in the overly full room.

"I'll say. That is one scary chick. Hot though. Is she seeing anyone?"

"Not as far as I know," Conryu said. "Though she has a thing for the Reaper, so you might want to keep that in mind if you ask her out."

He spotted Kelsie standing off to one side and waved her over. He hugged her and kissed her forehead. "You okay?"

She burrowed her head into his chest and nodded. A moment later tears soaked his shirt. "Hey, it's okay. You're safe now."

She sniffed. "I know. I'm just so relieved and ashamed at what my grandmother tried to get Heather to do."

"You should know I don't judge you by what Malice does. Don't give the old bat a second thought."

Kelsie finally smiled. "I won't."

"What now, dude?" Jonny asked.

"That's an excellent question. If no one actually needs medical attention, I'd say you should all stay here for the moment. There's a huge gun battle going on at the hotel entrance so it's not like you can leave. I'll go deal with those losers then come get you guys."

Kelsie looked at him with wide eyes. "You're going to leave us here?"

"Don't worry, Kai will be nearby. No one will even get close to you, I promise."

"Okay," she said.

"When you finish up, there's something we need to discuss," Maria said.

"Anything you want. I'll be back."

Conryu's smile withered when he turned away from his friends. Things could have gone so much worse than they did. Whoever the invaders were, he was going to make them pay. Maybe, just this once, he wouldn't hold back. If ever there was a group that deserved to have their souls devoured by the Reaper, it was this lot.

* * *

Lady Tiger limped along past rundown buildings, shacks, and dumps. Her whole world was pain, everything hurt, her shoulder, her back, her legs, everything. She focused through her misery, putting one foot in front of the other like a robot.

Every building on the street looked like its owner didn't know the meaning of the word maintenance. It wasn't the worst slum she'd visited in her career, but it ranked right up there. Despite the rundown appearance, the local landlords secured their property surprisingly well. Every door she tried was tightly locked.

She reached the end of the first block and still hadn't found a suitable place to hole up. Her trembling legs argued that maybe they could take a quick break. She ignored them. Lady Tiger feared that if she sat down, she'd never get up again.

She groaned and stumbled along on her quest for a hideout. What was she going to do? Father Salvador would be on her trail sooner rather than later. If she didn't find somewhere out of sight quick, she'd be out of luck. Lady Tiger paused to catch her breath and glanced across the street.

Her gaze landed on a warehouse, a small one, probably a wholesale business at one point, less than half the size of the buildings the Blessed Army had used as a base. What drew her attention wasn't the size, but the fact the door on the side of the building flopped back and forth in the light breeze. It was the only thing she'd seen remotely resembling a place to hide. It might not have been ideal, but she'd run out of options.

Mustering her strength, Lady Tiger limped across the street and went inside. Someone had busted the doorframe which explained why the door flapped around the way it did. The interior of the building matched the neighborhood perfectly. Smashed crates mixed with heaps of torn clothing and other assorted junk.

A quick search of the cluttered area inside turned up a length of string. It wasn't much, just a simple piece of nylon paracord. She looped it around the doorknob, pulled the door tight, and tied it off so it wouldn't swing around and draw attention she didn't want. Her solitary hope was that Father Salvador would overlook the building as nothing special.

But just in case he didn't, Lady Tiger drew the last of her reserves and sketched a ward just inside the door. It wasn't the most powerful defense she'd ever constructed, but whoever opened that door next would be in for a rude welcome. She'd done all she could, now it was time to find somewhere to rest.

Lady Tiger picked her way through the piles of garbage trying to find somewhere out of the way to lie down. She slumped on a filthy mattress hidden under a pile of broken pallets. Despite the urine stains and large cockroach crawling across it, it might've been the finest sight she'd ever seen. It looked like some vagrant had been using this as a temporary home. Probably the same person who broke the door. Hopefully he wouldn't return and set off her surprise.

Lady Tiger settled in and closed her eyes. She was so exhausted she didn't even care if someone found her. All she wanted to do was sleep. In moments she got her wish.

* * *

Once Conryu was out of sight of the hotel room, his expression grew cold. These sons of bitches tried to kill his friends and came near to succeeding. He couldn't allow that to happen again. He wouldn't allow it.

"Where are they, Prime?"

"One group of four is climbing the northern staircase. The lower floors are mostly empty of living people and the few that are there can't be distinguished between guests and marauders."

Of course they couldn't. That would have been too simple. When it came to sensing their life force, one human was much the same as another. He'd just have to clear the hotel one floor at a time. Shouldn't take long if he searched while remaining in Hell. It would've made a good job for Kai, but he wanted her to stay behind and protect the others. This was the first time he'd wished for an extra ninja on his team.

First things first. He turned toward the northern staircase. He'd deal with that group then clear the rest of the floors.

The wall of ice sealing the entrance to the floor had already melted down to little more than a puddle. With a wave of his hand Conryu dispelled the rest of the barrier. The thump of heavy tread was rapidly approaching and soon enough the first of the soldiers appeared below. The man spotted Conryu and raised his rifle.

With a thought Conryu reduced it to so many iron filings. Conryu leapt from the landing and slammed his fist into the unknown soldier's chin. With his Diamond Skin spell in effect, the blow landed like a sledgehammer. The soldier went down and didn't get back up. Directly behind him were three more men in black uniforms. They got off a few rounds before he disintegrated their weapons.

All three of them drew knives, as if those would do any good, and surrounded him. He let several blows land intentionally. His father would have had a fit if he'd seen that, but Conryu wanted them to feel as helpless as their victims. Twice more he let the razor-sharp steel skid across skin harder than granite.

When one of them tried to stab him in the chest, Conryu caught his wrist and squeezed. The bones crunched in his enhanced grasp.

He yanked the man towards him and head butted the soldier in the nose.

The heavy blow caved his opponent's whole face in.

The other two looked at each other and in their moment of hesitation he waded in, kicking one of them in the chest with enough force to lift him off his feet and send him flying down the steps.

Conryu uppercutted the second, snapping his head back, and sending him flying into the wall.

It took only a second to tell this lot wasn't a danger.

"Are there any more coming?" Conryu asked.

"No, Master," Prime said. "The next nearest human is eight feet below us and a hundred and twenty feet to your right."

Conryu nodded. "Reveal the way through infinite darkness. Open the path. Hell Portal!"

He stepped through into the endless darkness and closed the portal behind him. Cerberus came trotting up at once and barked at him. Conryu gave him an absentminded pat on the flank before opening a viewing window and easing his way down and to the right.

It didn't take long to find a family huddled alone in one of the rooms. They were hiding in the closet as if that would keep them safe should the soldiers show up. There was no threat there.

He continued floor by floor checking every room and finding nothing but scared guests. It looked like the invaders, whoever they were, had focused their efforts on trying to kill the families of wizards.

When he reached the lobby, Conryu found a war waiting for him. He'd known looking down from above that it was bad, but seeing it at eye level, even if he remained safe in another realm, took things to the next level.

Soldiers in black uniforms mixed with a random assortment of the worst-looking people you could think of. He imagined they'd emptied out a juvenile detention center. Everyone had at least a machine gun of some sort and many sported hand grenades dangling from their belts. A constant stream of bullets flew back and forth. There wasn't a safe place to be had in the lobby. Stepping out into that madness, even with this magical protection, would be risky.

Conryu retreated to a storage room out of sight of the invaders, left Hell, and was assaulted by near-deafening noise. The crack of machine guns and the explosions of grenades mingled with the shouts and swearing of the wounded. The noise hammered at his ears and made him wince.

He took a moment to consider the best way to deal with the terrorists and decided to try one of his new tricks. He drew a circle of dark magic and cast a summoning spell.

The circle became a disk and out of it stepped three black hounds. Flames dripped from their mouths and their eyes glowed red. Each beast resembled a miniature Cerberus with only one head and standing as tall as his elbow. The hell hounds all looked expectantly at Conryu.

He pointed at the lobby. "Take down anyone with a gun inside the building. Don't kill unless you have to."

The hell hounds growled and he took that to mean that they understood. Unlike some demons, they couldn't speak. Some people thought that made them stupid, but they were extremely intelligent. The spell, combined with their inherent obedience to Cerberus's master, would compel them to do as he said. Conryu snapped his fingers. That was all the signal they needed.

The hounds howled, sending a chill down his spine. How many beings, human or demon, had heard that sound before having their throat ripped out? He shuddered to think about it.

The hell hounds leapt out the door and into the lobby. New screams mingled with the clatter of weapon fire. It didn't take long before the guns grew quiet and cries from the dying took their place.

Conryu emerged from the storeroom and watched as hell hounds took down a man and bit his arm off at the elbow. It didn't even bleed as the flames they constantly generated seared the wound shut. It was brutal, but they were obeying his orders.

In less than five minutes all the enemy soldiers had fallen. The hell hounds padded over, their tongues lolling, and sat at his feet. He patted each of them on the head, scratched behind their ears, and said, "Good boys. I'll tell Cerberus how well you all did."

He opened a portal and sent them back to Hell.

"Master, people are coming."

Probably the Kingdom soldiers coming to see why no one was shooting at them anymore. Conryu put his hands up just as a camouflaged man with a machine gun burst through the door. Ten more came in behind him.

They looked around at the carnage filling the lobby and one by one fixed on Conryu. Eleven guns centered on his head and chest. Even with Diamond Skin protecting him that many weapons directed at him made Conryu nervous.

"On your knees! Now!" the first soldier shouted.

Conryu did as they ordered and was quickly surrounded. Prime stayed quiet and floated up near the ceiling.

"Identify yourself," the soldier said.

"Conryu Koda. I'm on the North American Alliance's team. When we found out what happened I came here as fast as I could. I've got friends upstairs."

The soldier grabbed his arm and pulled him to his feet. Most of the guns were now pointing at the floor.

The leader of the soldiers—he had some markings on his uniform, but Conryu didn't know what they meant—waved at the carnage. "You did this?"

"Not personally, but I summoned the hell hounds that did it."

"These bastards held us off for the better part of an hour and according to our spotters, you dealt with them in under three minutes."

Conryu nodded. "You're welcome. Can I go check on my friends now?"

"We need to clear the rest of the building to make sure it's safe," the officer said.

"I already checked it. There aren't any more— Say, just who are these people anyway?"

"Best as we can tell they're a mixture of local anarchists and Blessed Army fanatics. How they slipped into the Kingdom I have no idea, but I promise you heads will roll."

"Great. Am I under arrest?" Conryu asked.

One of the other soldiers came over and whispered in the officer's ear. "No, my man just confirmed your identity with the Ministry of Magic. I've been told to extend you every courtesy. I'll get those cuffs off you."

"That's okay." Conryu flexed and snapped the band, letting it fall to the floor. "I'll meet you upstairs."

He collected Prime, opened a Hell portal, and vanished into it.

* * *

Not wanting to startle his friends, Conryu stepped out of his portal well away from the room where he'd left the others. The hotel was safe for the moment. It took a weight off his mind. The next thing to do was find out if Mr. and Mrs. Kane were okay. Maria had to be worried.

He grimaced at the mess Kai left in the hall and picked his way through the bodies to the door. He knocked once and Maria opened it immediately.

She hugged him. "Is it over?"

"I don't know about over, but the hotel is secure. There are soldiers on the way, but they insisted on clearing the rest of the floors. I'm sure the other guests will be relieved to see them."

"I'm sure. Before they get here you and I need to talk." She wore a frown even deeper than the one she'd used when he told her about Heather paying him a late-night visit, so whatever she had on her mind must have been serious.

"What is it?"

Maria glanced into the room for a moment then back to him. "Heather tried to kill me."

"What!?" Everyone in the room looked his way. "Sorry."

"My back was to her, and she had a knife made of ice in her hand. If Kelsie hadn't dispelled it, Heather would've cut my throat. I knocked her out, but my spell's going to be wearing off soon. What are we going to do?"

"We're going to find out what the hell is going on, and if she doesn't tell us the truth I'll threaten to feed her to Cerberus."

"Maybe we shouldn't do this in front of everyone," Maria said.

"Good point. There are plenty of empty rooms. I'm sure any of those would do for an interrogation. I'll grab her and then we'll see what's what."

Conryu went in and scooped up Heather. A faint tingle ran through his arms, but he ignored it.

"Where are you taking her?" Kelsie asked.

"Just down the hall. We're going to have a little chat. Want to listen in?"

"I do," Kelsie said. She hopped up out of her chair and hurried over to the door.

"Me too," Jonny said.

The three of them joined Maria out in the hall and made the short walk to the next room. Conryu tossed Heather on the bed and dispelled whatever magic Maria had used to knock her out. Heather groaned and sat up.

She scrubbed a hand across her face and looked up at them. "Oh, God."

"You're going to need more help than that," Conryu said. "Why don't you tell us all about it and we'll decide what to do with you."

"I didn't want to do it. You have to understand, she forced me. It was my last chance to save myself. I'm not proud of what I did or, I guess, tried to do, but I didn't see any other way." Heather broke down and wept.

Normally the sight of a crying girl activated whatever it was that caused him to be so overprotective, but now he felt nothing. "So Malice put you up to it?"

"Yes, she thought with Maria dead you might end up with Kelsie and that would suit her plans quite well. I didn't really want to do it. You have to believe me."

"Grandmother told you to kill Maria in the hopes that Conryu and I would end up together?" Kelsie's disbelief came through loud and clear in her tone. The whole thing was beyond insane, but given Malice's involvement he shouldn't have been surprised.

Heather nodded, but didn't say anything.

Kelsie paced and ran her hands through her hair. She muttered unintelligibly, most likely about her grandmother. Conryu knew how she felt. He hated to see her so upset.

Unable to watch her anymore, he marched over and set himself in Kelsie's path. She practically ran into him before she stopped.

He put his hands on her shoulders. "It's not your fault. Your grandmother is a crazy, evil woman and what she does is not your responsibility."

Kelsie started crying. "But if we weren't friends, she wouldn't have thought killing Maria would accomplish anything."

"That just shows how insane she is. I don't blame you for

what happened and neither does anyone else. The most important thing is that you shouldn't blame yourself."

She hugged him and cried into his chest for a moment.
When she got herself under control, she stepped back. "Thank
you for that. What are we going to do about Grandmother?"

"That's an excellent question." Conryu turned to Heather.
"Will you testify to what she tried to make you do?"

"If you imagine I'm stupid enough to testify against Malice
Kincade, then you've got worse problems than I thought."

Conryu leaned down so that their faces were only inches
apart. "Let me rephrase. Are you willing to go to prison for
attempted murder rather than testify against her?"

Heather stared at him with wide eyes. Had she really not
thought about the consequences of her actions? "Suppose I
agree. What's to keep her from just having me killed?"

"What do you think will stop her from having you killed for
failing?" Maria asked. "At least if you agree to testify against
her the government might offer you some protection."

Heather hung her head. "How did it all go so wrong? This
was supposed to be an easy job, make some quick money, and
now I find myself in this position. I can hardly believe it."

"Yeah, you poor baby," Conryu said. "So what's it going
to be?"

"Alright, I'll do it."

Conryu nodded, surprised but pleased to hear her finally
willing to do the right thing. He felt like he owed her a little
something for that. "I promise I'll do what I can to protect
you."

"I doubt there's anything you can do, but I appreciate the
gesture."

11

DRIVE THEM OUT

When they finished their interrogation of Heather, Conryu and the others escorted her back to the room. The soldiers from downstairs stood outside in the hall waiting for them. If all the bodies bothered them, they gave no indication. After everything that had happened today, what was a few more corpses? The men looked a good deal more relaxed than they had in the lobby.

Their commander nodded to Conryu. "The other floors are secure, and we found no wounded. I sent a small team to check the top floor, but I don't expect any trouble."

"That's great, so what happens now?" Conryu asked.

"Funny you should ask. Director Simpson just arrived and requested that you come down and have a chat."

Conryu glanced at Maria and she nodded. He hated to leave his friends again, but they were as safe here as anywhere in the city. "I'll head down there now."

"If you want to save a walk, the elevators are working again," the commander said.

"Thanks for the heads up." Conryu walked over to the elevator bank and hit the call button. He selected the lobby and started down.

It took less than a minute to reach the ground floor. The door chimed and slid open. Conryu let out a sigh of relief when he spotted the Ministry director all by herself. He'd half feared to find Malice waiting with her. Conryu wasn't sure if he could've spoken to the woman without lashing out. He stepped out of the elevator and walked over.

"You wanted to speak to me, Director Simpson?" Conryu said.

"Jemma, please." She held out her hand and Conryu gave it a gentle shake. "First, I want to thank you for everything you've done here. Without your intervention things might've ended up much worse."

"I was happy to help. Is Mr. Kane and his wife okay? I never saw what happened to everyone else that was at the stadium."

"Everyone's fine. The terrorists didn't last long when the three teams outside of the competition grounds worked together to bring them down. The whole fight lasted about three minutes."

Some of Conryu's tension eased. Maria would be so relieved. "I'm glad to hear it. How are things in the rest of the city?"

"That's what I wanted to talk to you about. Our wizards are having a hard time dealing with so many attackers spread out all over the city. I was hoping you'd agree to lend us a hand in some of the heavier areas of fighting."

That was exactly what he expected her to say. Normally somebody asking him for something when he barely knew them would've annoyed Conryu, but under the circumstances he was glad to help.

"What do you need me to do?"

"They hit us in three main locations besides the hotel. The Ministry, Parliament, and in the skies above the city. If you can take out the dragon manes and knock out the heaviest clumps of fighting, it'll free up my people to hunt down any stragglers."

"I'll see what I can do," Conryu said. "Will you remain here or should I report in somewhere else?"

"I'll be here. Until the Ministry is cleared, we're going to use the hotel for a temporary base of operations. We'll be bringing any survivors here as well."

"Okay, I'll return as soon as I can."

Conryu marched out of the lobby, cast a flight spell, and leapt into the air. He didn't want to use Reaper's Cloak if he could avoid it, but he didn't know another way to handle the dragon manes quickly.

"Prime, is there an easy way to take out those dragons?"

"I assume you're seeking a lethal solution."

"Unless you know how to tame the creatures, I can't imagine another option that might work."

"No, Master, I'm afraid I don't. They aren't natural beasts and have no real place in the ecosystem."

"Then I guess lethal it is. What do you have?"

A faint tingle formed in the back of Conryu's mind and a moment later the words to a spell appeared. It was called Reaper's Touch and it basically mimicked what he did when wearing the cloak. Conryu frowned. He hated relying on the Reaper's power, but under the circumstances there was no real choice.

Less than a mile from the hotel he spotted the first of the dragon manes. It circled a damaged high-rise and breathed fire on it. A trio of Ministry wizards blasted away at it with lightning and ice to no effect. Conryu stopped, gathered himself, and chanted. "Hand of bone, touch of death, reach out and claim the life of my enemy, Reaper's Touch!"

A shadowy black hand flew out and slid into the dragon mane. It went rigid, glided for a few feet, and started to fall.

Conryu couldn't let the body hit anything. It had to weigh six tons. He focused on it and cast, "Shatter!"

The corpse crumbled to dust in an instant. One of the Ministry wizards flew over and said, "Thanks."

"No problem, Jemma sent me to lend you guys a hand. Have you seen the second one?"

"Damn thing flew east about five minutes ago. Haven't seen it since."

He hated to let one of the monsters get away, but didn't have time to hunt it down right now. "She said I was supposed to help out at the Ministry building and Parliament. How are things going there?"

"Afraid I haven't a clue, we've been pretty busy up here."

Looked like he was going in blind. "Fair enough. Can you point me towards Parliament?"

She gave him directions to both locations and Conryu got going. It was a fairly simple matter for him to use some of his more powerful spells to turn the tide at both locations the same as he had at the hotel. Half an hour later, he was on his way back.

He landed and strode into the lobby. Jemma didn't even give him a chance to sit down.

"We have another problem," she said.

Seemed like there was always another problem. "What's wrong now?" he asked.

"I just got word that the team transporting some elf artifacts to the museum was attacked and an item stolen."

Conryu tensed. "By a woman in a mask?"

"That's right, how did you know?"

"Call it a hunch." Damn the Society! They were using the chaos to steal another artifact. "What did she take?"

"That's the weird thing, all she took was a broken artifact."

The knot in Conryu's stomach felt like an elephant. Lady Wolf had taken a broken artifact from the czar's collection. It couldn't be a coincidence.

"Two of our wizards pursued her—there was an enchantment on the item that allowed them to track it—but we haven't heard from them in a while. Given the chaos in the city I'm not too surprised—"

"What was their last known location?" He needed to get his hands on the thief and make her tell him what they were up to. Conryu felt like he was constantly half a step behind the Society and he was sick of it.

She rattled off an address. "It's in the slums. I know we're not supposed to call it that, the proper term is economically challenged neighborhood, but it's a slum. Will you be able to find it okay?"

"Yeah, I've got a guide."

He opened a Hell portal and when Cerberus appeared told the demon dog the address. It was time to hunt.

* * *

The wind picked up as Father Salvador and his assistant worked their way down the street. He reached up to scratch the blistered skin on his cheek and his finger came back covered in dead skin. He'd gotten used to the pain; it hadn't lessened so much as become a part of him. He thought no more of it than he did his hand or foot.

The faint scuff marks they'd been following, assuming they even came from the witch, were now so smeared and vague he believed Jeremiah acted more on hope than tracking skill.

Or perhaps divine providence guided their path. It was God's will they find and destroy the witch. Perhaps he guided them on their mission. Yes, no other explanation made sense. His faith was being rewarded.

At least there were no people to hinder his search. The scum that lived in this wretched part of earth had either fled or locked themselves out of sight. Prudent decisions on their part. His allies were less than particular about who they firebombed. Though they did seem to prefer burning things of great value. That rendered this area far down on their target list.

They rounded a bend and Jeremiah placed a hand on his shoulder and pulled him behind the building they'd just passed.

"Look, Father." He pointed into the sky.

Salvador squinted. Two wizards in red robes he'd come to recognize as belonging to the Ministry circled above the block across the street. He raised his rifle partway then lowered it. Perhaps God had sent these hounds to guide him to his prey. How sweet it would be to have the heathens lead him to the one he sought. Surely the Almighty would appreciate the joke. He motioned Jeremiah further out of the way and settled in to see what happened.

The wait wasn't lengthy. The wizards dropped out of the sky and landed in front of the closed door of a small warehouse across the street. Nothing about the place struck Salvador as extraordinary. What did the wizards know that he didn't?

"What should we do, Father?"

"You should be silent."

He returned his attention to the wizards. They stood outside the door and put their heads together. Sometimes, not often, but sometimes, he wished his faith granted him some of the gifts the wizards enjoyed. Right now he would have given much to hear what they were discussing.

They appeared to reach a consensus. One stepped back while the other grasped the handle. She shoved the door open.

An explosion sent the door flying into the wizards. They sprawled on the ground with the shards of the door covering them.

Salvador knew a sign when he saw one. Raising his rifle, he charged across the street. His first shot scattered one wizard's brains all over the ground. A quick reload and he gave the second woman the same treatment.

He panted with a combination of exertion and divine exultation. Two fewer wizards now blighted the world with their presence. The one he really needed to kill still remained. Judging from the trap, she had to be inside. At last he would finish his prey and rejoin the greater battle.

Salvador slammed a third bullet into the chamber of his rifle and stepped into the warehouse.

* * *

Conryu stepped out of his portal across the street from the address Jemma had given him. It never ceased to amaze him how Cerberus knew exactly where to go. He was tempted to ask Prime how it worked, but he feared the scholomantic might tell him.

"Sense anything?"

"There are people everywhere, but I only detect three in the building across the street."

Conryu glanced up and down the empty block. Everywhere must mean inside. The area was so empty he expected a tumbleweed to go rolling past any minute.

"That must be Jemma's people and the Society wizard."

Prime flexed his cover. "There are three people, but I can't tell you who they are."

"Well, let's go take a look."

Conryu was barely halfway across the street when he spotted the two bodies. They wore the robes of Ministry wizards. He dashed over to help, but when he arrived found that their heads had both been blown to smithereens. It looked more like the damage of a bullet than a spell.

"Prime, is there any magic around them?"

"Dark magic, Master. I suspect someone has gotten their hands on some Death's Head bullets."

"Death's Head bullets?"

"Bullets enchanted to penetrate magical defenses. Be cautious, Master, Diamond Skin won't protect you from them."

Terrific. One more complication to add to the list. Did regular people feel like this when they had to deal with the various spells available to wizards? Well, just because his defensive spells wouldn't protect him from enchanted bullets was no reason to cancel any of them and give regular bullets a chance to hurt him.

Conryu put a finger to his lips and kneed the door open. The landing was charred from where a spell had detonated. He paused and listened. Farther into the junk-strewn building people were moving around.

He glanced up at the ceiling. It would be a lot easier to see anyone up there. The problem was he couldn't fly with an earth magic spell running. He debated for a moment whether it would be safer to stay on the ground or go into the air.

Finally, he released the protective spell and cast a flying spell. If their bullets could penetrate it anyway better to see them coming. He flew silently up into the rafters and immediately spotted two men working their way through the garbage. One of them carried a long rifle and the other had a submachine gun. Both wore black uniforms, Blessed Army then. They hadn't noticed Conryu yet so he let them do the searching for him.

They kicked over boxes and poked their noses in everything. For the better part of five minutes they looked high and low for the Society wizard. Finally they hurled a pair of pallets off to one side and there she was, passed out on the filthy mattress, her shoulder soaked with dried blood.

Conryu had never seen a member of the Society in such poor shape. Usually they were these arrogant, powerful women who looked down on him. This one wasn't in any shape to look down on anyone. For half a second he felt a little bad for her, but it didn't last.

The man with a long rifle raised his weapon and took aim at the unconscious woman.

Conryu descended and gathered his will. "Shatter."

Both men's weapons disintegrated. The moment he landed he renewed his defensive spell.

They turned to face him. The elder man, his face and chest horribly burned, said, "So you are the male wizard. I have heard of you. Are you allied with this wretch?"

Conryu offered a humorless laugh. "Hardly, but I have some questions for her and if you kill her, I'll have to resort to spells I don't especially enjoy casting. Is there any chance I can convince you to surrender?"

The younger man drew long daggers from sheathes at his waist.

"I'll take that as a no."

He charged and Conryu stepped right into him, driving his fist into the man's gut and doubling him over. A quick shove sent him sprawling to the floor.

Conryu cast, "Deepest cold, bind and hold, Ice Bind!"

Two inches of clear ice covered him and locked him in position. He turned his attention to the last man and found him running as fast as possible toward the door.

"Gust!" Winds screamed, picked the soldier up, and slammed him into the far wall where he slumped to the ground.

Finally. With those nuisances dealt with he could interrogate his prisoner in peace.

A boom shook the warehouse as a portal appeared. A woman in green robes wearing a dragon mask stepped out. It was the one that came to talk to him at Kincade Manor.

"I told you we'd see each other again," Lady Dragon said.

"So you did. I don't suppose this is where you explain your evil plot?"

She held out her hand and a crimson rod appeared. "No, I'm afraid not."

* * *

Lady Tiger never would've imagined she'd be glad to see Conryu Koda, but when he landed and distracted Father Salvador from shooting her, she couldn't have been more relieved. She'd faked being unconscious in hopes that he might take her prisoner instead of simply shooting her. When the rifle went up, she recognized her hope as a vain one. And then like a guardian angel, the Society's greatest enemy floated to the ground and saved her.

She used the distraction and the last speck of power in her to send a message to the Society requesting assistance. Oh, and how that galled her. The other Hierarchs would never let her live it down, but at least she might live. If those were her choices then reputation be damned.

Now Lady Dragon faced off against Conryu and the warehouse practically vibrated with their combined magical power. They exchanged words, she couldn't make out what they said, but a moment later they shot into the air and blasted through the roof.

Lady Tiger groaned. She'd survive for a few more minutes. Nearby a wind portal opened and Lady Wolf emerged. Her sister Hierarch walked over and looked down at her. Though the mask hid it, Lady Tiger pictured the sneer of contempt twisting Lady Wolf's lips.

She shook her head. "Pathetic. Did you complete your mission?"

"I did."

"Good. If Lady Dragon hadn't ordered it otherwise, I'd leave you here as just reward for your incompetence. She still seems to think we need you in order to complete the mission, so it's fallen to me to carry you to safety. Hold still."

Lady Wolf cast a spell and a disk of energy appeared under Lady Tiger. It lifted her off the filthy mattress. She choked off a scream when the movement jarred her shoulder. In moments she would be safe at the Society's headquarters. Lady Bear had a gift for light magic and her healing would see Lady Tiger well in short order.

Lady Wolf gestured and the makeshift gurney drifted along

behind her. They passed through the portal and Lady Tiger lost consciousness for real.

* * *

C onryu faced Lady Dragon in the skies above the London slum. Fire crackled around the red scepter she carried. He didn't recognize the artifact, but it didn't take a genius to know it served a similar purpose to the Death Stick. The only question was, how much did the item magnify her power? He guessed a lot. You didn't get to run an outfit like the Society without a great deal of power backing you up.

"I've been looking forward to testing your strength myself," Lady Dragon said. "You've caused us a great deal of trouble, but that all ends now."

"You think it'll be that easy?" He didn't really care about her answer, he just wanted to give Prime a chance to get as far away as their connection allowed. He wasn't completely confident in his ability to protect the scholomantic, even with their shared Cloak of Darkness.

"Let's find out." Lady Dragon flourished the scepter and a river of flame rushed toward Conryu.

He threw up a hand and shouted, "Break!"

His spell blew away a chunk of the flames, but they kept coming. Relying on nothing but instinct and willpower, he transformed the sphere of dark magic into a wall. It blocked every drop of flame and when he sensed the torrent had ended, he lowered it.

"Is that the best you've got?" he asked.

He sensed her smiling behind the mask. "I'm just getting warmed up."

The two opponents circled. Lady Dragon attacked with fire

and lightning. Conryu countered with Dispel and blasts of ice. Neither of them landed a solid strike.

The first hint of a backlash headache was forming behind Conryu's eyes when a fireball twice the size of his head came roaring in.

He hollowed it out with a Dispel and flew through the gap. On the other side Lady Dragon panted and leaned with her hands on her knees. Looked like he wasn't the only one getting low on power. He'd been fighting all afternoon. What was her excuse?

If he pushed hard, maybe he could end this now. Sensing his need, Prime sent power rushing down their link. His headache vanished and he cast, "Shroud of all things ending. Cowl of nightmares born. Dark wrap that looks upon all things' doom, Reaper's Cloak!"

The shroud fell into place.

Conryu flew toward Lady Dragon, no longer worried about what her spells might do to him.

Lady Dragon raised her scepter.

Light gathered at the tip and exploded in a blinding flash. Within the protection of the cowl he felt no discomfort, but the glare blocked his view.

He waved his hand and it vanished, just in time for him to watch her vanish into a portal. The glowing disk disappeared, leaving him alone in the sky.

Conryu silently cursed the Society as he let his spell fade away. He descended through the hole in the roof and found the other one gone as well. She hadn't been trying to win, only keep him busy while her flunkies retrieved his prisoner.

"Damn them all!" He kicked a box and sent it flying across the room.

"It could be worse, Master," Prime said.

"How?"

"She might have killed you."

He stared at his scholomantic for a moment then barked a humorless laugh. "You've got me there, pal. Let's tie these nuts up and get back to the hotel. If the powers that be have any more jobs, they can get someone else to handle them."

EPILOGUE

ozens of cars and buses surrounded the hotel when he returned. Just as Jemma said, it appeared the entire Kingdom government had set up shop there. He landed outside the entrance and after a glaring contest with a pair of soldiers on guard duty was let in.

A sea of people, most of them dressed in uniforms or suits, filled the lobby. All the bodies had been cleared and temporary tables loaded with computers brought in. The drone of voices put his teeth on edge. Ten feet from the door he found Grant waiting, his formerly crisp uniform now wrinkled and sweat stained. Looked like he'd seen a bit of action.

"Welcome back, sir."

"Grant. You're looking a little worse for the wear. You okay?"

"Perfectly, sir. Let me take a moment to say how sorry I am. I fear as a bodyguard I was an abject failure."

"Don't take it too hard. Having regular soldiers try to

protect wizards that can fly and travel through portals isn't the best idea. Have you seen Jemma? I've got some news for her, not much of it good."

"Jemma, sir?"

Conryu forced himself not to laugh at Grant's expression. "Director Simpson of the Ministry of Magic. Never mind, I see her."

Jemma was pacing and waving her arms at a pair of women in matching red robes. Conryu wove his way around the various stations that had been set up and waited for her to notice him. It didn't take long.

She waved her subordinates away and they ran off before she changed her mind. "What news, Conryu?"

He gave her the short version of his encounter at the warehouse. When he finished he said, "I'm sorry about your people."

Her expression grew cloudy for a moment, but it passed quickly. "They won't be the only members of the Ministry mourned today. I'll send someone over straight away to collect your prisoners. You have my most sincere thanks for everything you've done. Ninety percent of the fighting was wrapped up minutes after you broke their backs at Parliament and the Ministry building. We should have the city under control by the end of the day."

"That's good. Sorry about the second dragon mane. Maybe it'll get tired halfway across the ocean and drown."

"We can only hope. I'm sure you must be tired. Your friends are still upstairs. Please consider your day's work complete." She held out her hand and he shook it. "The Kingdom owes you a great debt, Conryu. We won't forget what you've done here."

He nodded and made his way to the elevators. Noon hadn't

even arrived and he felt like he'd been fighting for days. The door slid open and he stepped in. Grant made a move to join him, but Conryu held up a hand. "How about we call it good? I'm just going to spend the rest of the day hanging out with my friends."

Grant smiled. "Fair enough, sir. Good luck to you."

They shook hands and Conryu rode up on his own. When he reached the second-to-last floor and left the elevator it came as a pleasant surprise to find all the bodies removed from the hall. It appeared someone had been busy.

Maria sat talking with her parents when he arrived. Sonja was still sound asleep and off to one side Jonny and Kelsie had a card game going. Of the other survivors there was no sign. Hopefully they'd been reunited with their families.

Mr. Kane spotted him first and waved him over to the bed. "Good to see you're okay, Conryu."

Conryu choked back the first reply that came to mind. Mr. Kane couldn't have known he was sending Conryu into a war zone. It was just bad luck that things had turned out the way they did. "Likewise. How bad was it?"

Mr. Kane looked away then back. "Bad. You and Crystal got lucky. The others all lost at least one member of their family. Two of the girls on the Australian team lost both parents. It was an absolute bloodbath. I wish there was something we could do for them, but our time in the Kingdom is up. We're heading home tomorrow."

Conryu was happy to hear it. His time as a media figure couldn't end fast enough. Hopefully the Department would let him beg off even joining the team next year, though it would be nice to visit the Empire of the Rising Sun which was due to host the tournament next year.

* * *

That night, Conryu's sleep was troubled by nightmares, most of them featuring women in masks torturing him. No great surprise there. When he woke up for the third time, the sun was just peeking out from between a pair of still-smoking skyscrapers. He couldn't see any point in trying to get back to sleep so he climbed out of bed, dressed, and finished packing. Their flight left at nine that morning, so he didn't have a lot of time to fool around.

At seven he rode the elevator to the lobby and found Maria waiting off to one side away from the others who had come down to meet the bus. She sat at the same table where he'd told her about Heather. Somehow the similarity did nothing to reassure him.

"What are we going to do?" Maria asked as soon as he sat down. "She tried to kill me once, what's to keep her from trying again?"

"After Heather testifies, there's no way Malice will try anything else. She'd be the first one the police looked at. She might be evil, but she's not stupid. Did you tell your parents?"

She stared at him like he'd lost his mind. "Are you crazy? Who knows what she might do if Dad raises a stink? He'd lose his job at the very least. And Mom... No, no. We'll keep this between you and me for now."

Conryu wanted to argue that it might be better if her parents heard about it from her rather than from a detective, but he wasn't inclined to argue with her. "If that's your call, I'll follow your lead. I'll maybe have a little talk with Malice before we leave. I doubt it'll do much good, but I've got to try."

She leaned across and kissed his cheek. "I know. Just don't do anything crazy."

He grinned. "Who, me?"

"Yeah, you." She gave him a better kiss.

More people had gathered in the lobby while they were talking so they went to join them. Maria broke away to stand beside her parents while Conryu hung back and looked for Malice.

Ten minutes before they were due to leave she emerged from one of the elevators, her two toadies alongside. Conryu gritted his teeth and marched over to talk to her. He hated this sort of thing, but damned if he was going to let her try to kill Maria and not say anything.

He stopped dead in her path and looked from one flunky to the other. "Get lost. I need to talk to your boss."

The two women glared at him and didn't so much as flinch.

He turned his attention to Malice. "Do you want to discuss this in front of them?"

"Discuss what?" Malice asked, a faint smile tugging at the corner of her lips.

"Heather James, and an unfortunate near accident. We had a long chat and she'll be having another one with the authorities in Central when we get home."

Malice barked a laugh and motioned for Thing One and Thing Two to run along. When they'd moved out of hearing distance she said, "I am the authority in Central. I assure you anything that pathetic whore has to say will fall on deaf ears. Now get out of my way."

She took a step, but Conryu didn't move. "If her words don't impress you then listen to me. If anything happens to Maria, it will be the last thing you ever do in this world. I don't care who you are or how many friends you have in high places. They won't be enough to protect you."

Malice just shook her head. "We both know you don't have

the stomach to kill me. Don't make threats you can't carry out. It's pitiful."

"Oh, it's not me that's going to come for you. Kai."

She had half a moment of confusion before the black blade of Kai's sword slid around her neck and rested against the wrinkled skin.

"I've made some new friends this year. The one holding your worthless life in her hands is Kai. And while you're right about my distaste for killing, I assure you she has no such compunction. I'm going to say this once more, slowly, so you're sure to understand. Stay away from Maria, her parents, my parents, and my other friends. If anything happens to any of them I'm holding you responsible. One word from me and you're dead. Understand?"

He didn't wait for an answer. A nod sent Kai back to the borderlands before he turned and walked away. Hopefully the hag would take the hint and leave them all alone.

* * *

In the council chamber of the Society's home base, Lady Dragon sat at the head of the table with Ladies Wolf, Bear, and Lion looking fixedly at the two fragments of the elf artifact sitting side by side, their jagged ends not quite touching. It had been a simple thing to remove the tracking spell the Ministry put on their half.

Lady Tiger remained unable to join them as she was still in a light magic healing field. According to Lady Bear, the weapon used to inflict the wound in her shoulder also created a barrier to magical healing so her recovery was proceeding at a snail's pace.

"Why did we even bother to bring Lady Tiger back?" Lady

Wolf asked. "She already demonstrated her incompetence, surely we'd be better off finishing her and elevating one of our other members in her place."

"Our Sub-Hierarchs have been decimated and of the regular members, none even come close to Lady Tiger's power," Lady Dragon said. "Despite her failings, we still need her to complete our task. It will take all of us working together to repair the artifact.

A moment of silent contemplation passed then Lady Bear asked, "Mistress, what does the device do?"

Lady Dragon gave her a sharp look.

"Not that I don't trust your judgement," Lady Bear hastened to add. "But I'm sure we're all curious to know now that we have both pieces."

"I should have thought that would be obvious to everyone," Lady Dragon said. "What keeps us from rescuing Morgana? Or for that matter what keeps our mistress from blasting her way out of her prison?"

"Magic doesn't work on The Lonely Rock," Lady Wolf said.

"Exactly." Lady Dragon chose to ignore her subordinate's less than respectful tone. "Or perhaps more precisely the tiny portals we open when we draw on the magical realms' energy refuse to open on the island. The artifact we've gone to so much trouble to recover is a mobile portal. It can be aligned to a single element and an aligned wizard can draw power through it."

A gasp went around the table as the others realized what that meant.

"I can't begin to imagine why the elves had need of such a device," Lady Dragon continued. "Perhaps on their world such magic dead zones were more common, a horrifying thought if ever there was one. Whatever their reasons for creating it, the artifact will allow us to finally rescue Morgana. And once she's free, let the world tremble."

So we've come to the end of our most recent story. I hope you enjoyed reading it as much as I enjoyed writing it. Only one book left and with the sinister LeFay Society on the verge of completing their dark plans you can be sure things are only going to get worse for Conryu and the gang in the final book. I hope you'll join me next time for the final installment of The Aegis of Merlin Series.

Thanks for reading,

James E. Wisher

ABOUT THE AUTHOR

James E. Wisher is a writer of science fiction and Fantasy novels. He's been writing since high school and reading everything he could get his hands on for as long as he can remember. This is his seventeenth novel.

To learn more:

www.jamesewisher.com

james@jamesewisher.com

Made in the USA
Monee, IL
12 April 2021